In My Father's
Image

By Robert Saunders

Published by:

P.O. Box 1746, New York, NY, 10017
Phone: 718-498-2408 Fax: 718-498-2408
www.anewhopepublishing.com
email: NewHopePublish@aol.com

Library of Congress Catalog Card Number:

ISBN: 1-929279-06-X

Cover Design: Keith Saunders
            MarionDesigns@bellsouth.net
Copy Edit: Marlon Green
            Marlonwriter@yahoo.com

Printed by: Phoenix Color Corp.
            Nancey Flowers
            Phone: 212-936-7300 ext. 2299

Hope C. Clarke's Trilogy III

Not With My Son
(originally published as Pent-Up Passion)

Keesha Smalls has been out of passion's game for a long time until she takes a second look at her best friend's son.

The dashingly gorgeous Chris Walker brings more than flaming romance to Keesha's bedroom. Their secret romance is perfect until Christine, Chris' mother, finds out.

A mother's rage can be terrifying but someone's past can be deadly. Keesha learns that sometimes it's better to not know love than to love the wrong man.

ISBN: 0-9722771-5-3 $14.95

Vengeance Is Mine

One of the most horrifying moments of Chris Walker's life was when he found his mother murdered at the hands of his ex-girlfriend, Michelle Tanner. Now he has an even greater fear-she was just paroled from a 10-year prison sentence and is after his daughter...their daughter.

For 10 years Michelle Tanner has planned and waited patiently for this moment and there is no way she can fail:

"What I have given in love, I now take with revenge."

Vengeance Is Mine is riveting, shocking, and has five times the passion, deceit, and confusion of its predecessor Not With My Son.

ISBN: 0-979279-03-4 $14.95

Carrying Momma's Baggage

Chris Walker will have one last battle to save his daughter from inheriting her mother's proverbial baggage, but this time it's not just his daughter caught up in Michelle's sinister ploy. Marriages and friendships will be put to the ultimate test as Ashley unravels the emotions everyone has struggled to hide, and now that she's opened it, there's no going back!

Carrying Momma's Baggage brings a shocking but satisfying conclusion to the dynamic 'Not With My Son, Vengeance Is Mine' trilogy.

ISBN: 0-929279-04-3 $14.95

Shadow Lover
by Hope C. Clarke

A brutal beating and a miraculous surgery leaves behind a trail of bodies as an angry husband goes out on a binge to reclaim his escaped wife.

A surgeon's love and compassion will lead him to risk it all to protect her...maybe even with the lives of his medical staff. But can he protect her when there are no more bodies between them?

Shadow Lover is a riveting tale of passions, fears and choices.

ISBN: 1-929279-00-0 $14.95

Best Seller
by Hope C. Clarke
(October 2004)

Kurt Daley, an aspiring writer gets more than she bargains for when her favorite best-selling author, Dean Koontz hands her a possession he is dying to pass on.

Dean's new protégé, Kurt will fulfill her destiny and write the greatest best-seller ever—a dreadful tale that reaches out and touches everyone close to her. It isn't long before the accomplished writer finds herself living out a perilous tale of her own.

Now, Kurt Daley will have to find the secrets hidden behind being a best seller before the clock runs out. What if you knew that every page you wrote brought you closer to your end?

ISBN: 1-929279-06-X $14.95

*P*rologue

*A*nnette leaned her right side against the tub waiting for her equilibrium to return. She felt her left hand pressing down hard on a few pebble-like objects which she soon realized were her missing front teeth. Her head was throbbing, her eyes were heavy and the mere thought of what took place moments ago—or so it seemed, left an overwhelming urge to throw up, but she decided against it out of fear of what Melsean might do next. Every so often, her eyes would glaze over or attempt to roll behind her head, but she fought the urge to escape her painful existence. *How could he do such a thing to me and call himself a man of God*, she thought. *He's merely the opposite. Surely, he must be the Son of Satan.* Slipping in and out of consciousness, she began to mentally play back the events that led to her unfortunate position...

One

*A**nnette* flashed back to a half-hour prior to the kitchen where she was preparing supper for her and Melsean. It was supposed to be a nice, quiet evening spent eating then watching *Sampson*, his favorite movie, and hopefully get a little hard loving later. She took all necessary precautions to make this night special. She made a honey-lime-marinated roast duck, wild rice and a side dish of steamed-buttered baby carrots and asparagus spears. To top the evening off, she began preparing a black forest cake for dessert, frosted and topped with whipped cream and cherries. She wasn't worried about it going to waste because she expected her nephews over tomorrow for the Spring break vacation. In the midst of her blending the heavy cream, she never heard Melsean enter the apartment.

He was instantly greeted by the sweet aroma

coming from the kitchen and he swiftly advanced toward it like a cat. On his way there, he surveyed every square inch of the place. He peered into the kitchen and watched Annette as she blended the cream on the island counter while singing Linda James' greatest hit *Hypnotized.*

God she's beautiful, he thought to himself as he stared at her long, flawless legs that trailed to a place he longed to enter, but knew the Good Lord forbid it. As much as he desired this sexual good-ness, he knew he could never come to know her flesh. For sure, she was the very essence of Sodom and Gomorrah and he feared turning into a pillar of salt if he dared to gaze upon her naked temple in which God wished to destroy.

Today, Annette was wearing an extra micro-mini that just barely covered her enormous, yet firm, buttocks and left little if nothing to the imagination. Melsean was about to reach out and hug her from behind when he was interrupted by an inner-voice that was unfamiliar to him. It recited a scripture that was all so familiar.

Come away from her, my people, that you may not participate in her sins, neither be visited by her plagues. "Revelations, eighteenth chapter, verse four," he said silently, though loud enough to get Annette's attention.

"Melsean! I didn't hear you come in. Why are you sneaking around?"

He snapped back to reality. "I'm sorry, I thought you heard me, being I called your name six times," he said, peering over her shoulder. "I guess you couldn't hear me with all this racket you got going on in here. What are you making?"

"Oh, something special for my big boy, but you'll have to wait until I've finished cooking to find out."

"Hmm, fair enough, but whatever it is, it smells wonderful."

"You're not about to hit me with that 'you didn't have to do all this for me' bullshit, are you?"

"No, I just thought we'd agreed that we were okay with the simple and nothing too outlandish."

"That's true, we did, but I don't consider me making a home-cooked meal and dessert for my man complex or outlandish. If anything, it's a natural gesture expressed from one mate to their significant other of how much they appreciate their presence. And you have surely been an asset to me since my nasty separation with my husband, who just up and left."

"*Judging by the way you're dressed, I can see why,*" Melsean's inner-voice coaxed.

"And I don't know where I'd be if you didn't come when you did."

Probably in a dumpster.

The mere thought of what his inner-voice said brought a mischievous smile across his face.

"There's that smile that I love so much," she said as she advanced on Melsean, grinding her pelvis roughly against his swollen member as if it was possible to conjoin through fabric.

He felt his soldier rising to the command of her sexual prowess, but was startled by the voice in his head.

"Come away from her for her sins have piled up to reach heaven and God has remembered her crimes. Repay her as she has paid; give her even double for what she has done; in the capsule mixed, mix her a double portion. As she has glorified herself and lived in sensuality, to that measure impose on her torture and grief."

"What are you talking about?" Annette said, snapping him out of his fugue state.

"Huh, what?"

"Huh, my ass. You started quoting some shit from the Bible again. Last week when we got together, I tried to get close to you and you did the same thing. We've been seeing each other for three months, Melsean. Now that may not constitute a trouble sign to you, but the word fruit seems to jump in my head when I think about it."

"I'm not a homosexual and I would appreciate it if you would keep your blasphemous statements to yourself."

"Keep my blasphemous...What type of talk is that? I just spent three fucking hours preparing a meal for you," she said, holding three fingers close enough to Melsean's eyes to poke him in them. "Not to mention the first twenty hours marinating the duck I roasted for your ass. And another thing, this is my fucking house and I'll curse or say what I want when I goddamn feel like it!"

Melsean had a look of disdain on his face. His respect for this woman was swiftly dwindling, for in his twisted mind, she had blown his actions out of proportion. "Listen, I can't be around you when you act like this. It's unhealthy."

"No, Melsean, what's unhealthy is to let all this," she said gesturing to the food she prepared, "and this," groping his hard-on, "go to waste."

Melsean, with his face impassive, stared blankly at Annette as if for the first time seeing her for what she truly was.

"Because in her heart she says 'I sit as queen; I am no widow, and shall never see sorrow. Therefore on a single day her plagues shall be upon her, pestilence, mourning, famine and with fire shall she be burned up. For the Lord God who judges her is mighty," he said reaching into the counter drawer and pulling out a bottle of lighter fluid and a box of matchsticks.

"What are you talking about and what're you going to do with those?" she asked with a slight touch of apprehension and fear. She focused on the perspiration flowing down her back and collecting between her massive cheeks.

"What I'm talking about is Revelations, eighteenth chapter, verses seven through eight," he chided. "And what I'm going to do with these is end your sickness like the Good Lord commands. As you know, fire purifies the filthiest of things. C.D.C, that's the Center of Disease Control in case you didn't know, uses fire to contain, control and combat deadly viruses. I intend to cure you and I will, as sure as Jesus cured the man in Gerasenes that was possessed with demons, casting them into a herd of swine. Jesus asked him 'What is your name?' He said

'Legion' because many demons had entered him as they have entered you," he said pointing accusingly toward Annette with the hand that possessed the lighter fluid and began dousing her with it.

Finally comprehending what was about to take place, she flung the hot, fresh vegetables at Melsean's face, but miscalculated and barely made contact with his shoulder. This upset Melsean who was now completely under the control of his inner-mysterious partner.

"The kings of the Earth, who committed forni-cation and were wanton with her, shall weep and beat their breast over her, when they look at the smoke of her conflagration." He began reaching for a matchstick to strike, but before he could make contact, Annette forced the box out of his hand while kneeing him in the groin in the same motion and racing out of the kitchen.

Her first instinct told her to make a run for the door, but she realized it had at least four locks on it, excluding the deadbolt. Her second instinct advised her to run upstairs to her room, make a wedge in the door, lock it, and run to the phone and call for help. Out of both options, she decided to go with the lat-ter, racing upstairs toward the bedroom.

She made it as far as the first landing before Melsean was on her heels. He grabbed her by the ankle with a sweeping motion causing her to fall against the carpeted steps, but barely absorbed the shock of her impact. The force knocked the wind out of her as Melsean crawled his way on top of her. She flailed her arms wildly, attempting to hold Melsean off long enough to get her second wind. Sensing her motives, Melsean smashed his elbow into her face ending whatever hope she had of escaping.

Annette was jerked from her state of reminiscence when Melsean splashed some liquid over her. At first she thought it was water until she found herself stifled by the acrid odor of the lighter fluid. She stared at the chiseled body of her predator that seemed to contract with every heave of his lungs. Moving upward, her eyes stopped on the cold and blank look on Melsean's face as his hazel eyes stared back, causing Annette to broaden her eyes with awe.

"Why are you doing this?" she asked, trying to steady herself against the bathtub, searching with her eyes for anything she could use as a weapon to hold this beast at bay, but found none to her avail.

Melsean, again sensing her intentions, wagged his index finger in a tsk, tsk manner, making the sound effects for it by striking his tongue against the roof of his mouth, and then said, matter-of-factly, "Oh, I took the liberty of removing everything that could be considered or used as a weapon. Besides, you wouldn't want to strike a man of God, would you?"

At that point, Annette could see that a change was taking place in Melsean. His eyes became distant and were replaced by something more hideous than any she'd ever beheld. His face contorted and writhe, not fully metamorphosing, but enough for her to recognize the evil he harbored within. It was that moment that Annette knew her bathroom was going to be her grave. The reality of what was to come caused Annette's muscles to give way, forcing her urine and feces out; soiling herself. Like a gazelle trapped in the mighty claws of a lion, Annette submitted to the inevitable, but prayed that God would make her suffering as quick and painless as possible.

Melsean backed up to the entrance of the bathroom, reached for a matchstick, struck it against the flint, moved it in the symbol of a crucifix, and began quoting from Revelations again. "Standing at a considerable distance dreading her torture, they shall exclaim, 'woe, woe, for the great city of Babylon the mighty city'." He tossed the match. "For her judgment is come in a single hour."

Annette's body ignited, causing her to cringe in pain, but she refused to give him pleasure by crying out to the heavens.

"And the Earth's merchants will weep and mourn over her. The fruit for which your soul longed is out of your reach; all the elegance and the glitter you enjoyed are lost to you and never again will they be found."

She finally lay still in a heap of burning flesh, and Melsean raised his hands to the heavens and bellowed out with a mighty voice, "She is fallen, fallen, Babylon the great! She has become a resort for demons; a haunt for every unclean spirit; a refuge for every filthy and detested bird. For all nations have drunk of the wine of her passionate immorality and the kings of the Earth have committed fornication with her, and the merchants of the Earth have grown rich on her abundance of wantonness."

Melsean was so caught up in his actions that he never heard the riot squad break down the door and enter the apartment. They raced up the stairs following the rank odor of burning flesh, stopped at the top of the stairs, positioned themselves in every perimeter, and surrounded the perpetrator. When everyone was in their respective place, Sergeant McCray, who was leading the platoon, yelled to the perpetrator in a raspy voice.

"This is the police! You are tightly surrounded. Drop your weapon, put your hands behind your head, and walk backwards until told otherwise. Do you understand?"

Melsean ignored the cop's rhetoric and continued to watch the charred corpse as its remaining flesh burned and folded in on itself like paper in extreme heat. He was mesmerized by the different colors of light that danced within the fire. "Scribes and the Pharisees brought a woman caught in the act of adultery and placing her in the centre, they said to Jesus 'they were talking to test him so they might trump up a charge against him;' teacher, this woman was caught in the very act of adultery. Now, Moses ordered in the law to stone such as she, so what do you say?"

"This is your last warning. Drop your weapon, put your hands behind your head, and walk backwards until told otherwise," Sergeant McCray said more aggressively.

"But Jesus stooped down and wrote with his fingers on the ground;" Melsean knelt down and begun making drawings in the soot of his victim, "And when they kept questioning him, he raised himself and told them, 'let the sinless one among you throw the first stone at her.'"

With that said, Melsean swung around, raising himself at the same time facing the officers, and was greeted by six shots that tore through his chest, missing vital organs by centimeters, but enough to incapacitate him.

Melsean looked up to the ceiling as if staring beyond it and cried to his inner self; "Don't leave me. Please don't leave me now. All I've done, I've done for you. Am I not in your favor?"

The inner voice responded to him by saying, "How long have I been with you without your knowing me? I am going away to prepare a place for you. And when I have gone and have prepared a place for you, I will come again and take you to myself, so that where I am, you also will be, and where I am going you'll know the way."

Ah, John, fourteenth chapter, versus two through four, I know it well, Melsean thought. Comforted by his Lord's words, he closed his eyes. No longer subdued by the pain from his gunshot wounds, he drifted into a void where pain could torment his flesh no more.

Sergeant McCray moved towards the suspect in a crouching manner. When he got close enough, he used one foot to step on Melsean's wrist, prying the bottle of water out of it. Then he used the same procedure to remove the toothpicks from his other hand.

Two

Isabella woke up to the symphony of Bette Midler's *Wind Beneath My Wings* that came on every time her phone rang. She reached over to her nightstand retrieving the noisy contraption and pressed talk. "Hello?"

"Hey, Isabella, it's me, Kayman."

I know it's you. What I don't know is why you're calling me on my day off," she said sardonically.

"I'm sorry. I didn't mean to intrude, but I've been trying to reach you all week. I guess you haven't seen the news all week either, huh?"

"No, can't say that I did," she said, recalling her full week of binge drinking and partying like it was her last. She chuckled to herself, wincing at the pain she felt in her head. "I've got a splitting headache and please don't ask me why because this conversation already seems like it's going to drag its feet to the point and force me out of my bed."

"Well, you're right about the last part. It does

require you to get out of bed, but it won't take as long to explain as you think."

"Okay. So let's stop playing the dialogue game and get to the point."

"As you wish, your highness. Last week on Tuesday, a man was shot multiple times and arrested for turning his girlfriend into human pyrotechnics. So far they have no motive for his action. However, it seems our friend here has friends in high places. Guess who?"

"Kayman!"

"Sorry, it's Shuster and Johnson. And get this, they paid three point seven million dollars to our firm to defend him."

"Get out! This guy must be very valuable to them to spend those kinds of Benjamins."

"Yeah, well, that's were it gets tricky. You see, they've placed specific requirements to the handling of their money and our firm gets the account on two conditions."

"Oh, and who and how many are going to have to lap dance with this guy?"

"Just one—you."

"Me?" she said sounding a little perplexed.

"I mean you don't have to sleep with him. They want you to be his counsel and defend him."

Isabella raised herself off her pillow until she was sitting in a ninety-degree position, "And what's the second condition to this decent, yet indecent proposal?"

"Well, that's the other tricky part—you have to get the man off."

"Oh, come on, Kayman. They know that's impossi..."

"Wait, there's more. Upon the completion of your getting him off, not only will they hand over thirty-six accounts of their neighboring corporation to do business with us, but they also intend to give you another two point six million as a bonus for a job well done."

She thought over the information she was hearing. She could definitely use the money, not that she was an extravagant spender, but damn if she didn't love her Armani pant suits and Minolo leather pumps. The only thing that worried her was the obvious.

"And what if I can't come through for the defendant and they find him guilty?"

"Don't even think thoughts like that. Besides, Shuster and Johnson have complete faith in your getting Mr. Natas off and they refuse to accept another counselor to defend their employee. Of course, the term they used to define me and other attorneys was 'ordinary street lawyers' and the boss agrees. So like it or not, you're stuck with this client, Issey."

"Very well, but I don't have to like this—and I don't. When do I start?"

"Actually, you were supposed to be in court thirty minutes ago, but I've submitted an injunction to push it back for later, so you have to be in court for arraignment at one o'clock. I suggest you fix yourself a nice cup of black coffee on the go and get your high yella' ass over here."

She laughed out loud as she hung up. She loved when Kayman talked dirty to her. They were friends for a very long time and been through some tight situations. They had sex once in the course of their friendship, but decided early in the relationship, or at least she did, that their compatibility stopped at friendship and no further. She hurried to the bathroom, jumped in the shower, and cranked that baby on steam, and began lathering her body with a pear fragranced body wash she bought from the Body Shop located on 34th Street in Penn Station.

Twenty minutes later, she was fully dry, freshly scented with lotion, and adorned in a wine-colored silk underclothes set that accentuated her every bump and curve. Next, she opened her walk-in closet, searching through her limitless collection of suits, deciding on a wine-colored blouse, a black cotton pantsuit with a pair of Minolo three-inch strapless pumps. Finally, she grabbed a pair of natural-colored tights and left her closet, and proceeded to spray on her favorite perfume—Anais Anais. After completing that task, she grabbed her Christian Dior bag and keys and headed for the front door. Upon opening it, she reached down, retrieving her morning paper as she advanced to her 2004 Range Rover. Today's drive to work seemed longer than most she's had. Maybe it was the anxiety she felt about the task at hand. Now that she thought about it, she should have asked Kayman to have her client's file out for her so that she could review it before making her way to court, but then again, knowing Kayman, he probably took the initiative of doing it anyway.

About twenty-five minutes later, she was parking in the garage below the office building. She turned off the ignition, got out dragging her purse, locked up, and secured the alarm system on her way to the elevator. When inside, she pressed the button for the thirtieth floor, leaned back against the wall, and waited for her stop. When the indicator above struck thirty, the elevator came to an abrupt end, throwing its doors open and exposing four thousand square-feet of space filled with cubicles, offices, and suites. Each office was controlled by Riengold and Finkelstein's most prestigious employees and were assets to the company's financial growth. Isabella made her way to her suite and was greeted by her secretary Rhonda.

"Good morning, Ms. Danpier. You alright?" she said noticing the dark lines under Isabella's eyes.

"Good morning, Rhonda. Yes, I'm fine, but please stop calling me Ms. Danpier. I prefer Isabella."

"Yes, ma'am, Ms. Da—I mean, Isabella," she said coyly.

"See, doesn't that have a better ring than that 'Ms. Ma'am' bullshit?"

"Yes. It actually does, but it's going to take some time to get used to."

"Well, don't let it take too much time. It's not like we're spring chickens," she said as she nudged Rhonda causing her to giggle. "Okay, back to business. Do I have any calls?"

"Only the normal clients. One from Rene' Zellman, two from Jonathan Fienholtz, and one from Denmark Aires' offshore representative who said she'd call back later around noon. Oh, before I forget, Mr. Le'bron left your client Melsean Natas' file. He said if you came in and jumped right on it, you'd have enough time to familiarize yourself with the case and design your strategy for your one o'clock court appearance."

"Thank you, Rhonda. Anything else?"

"No, not unless you want to discuss lunch plans. But it appears that you're going to have your hands full for a while, so rain check?"

Definitely a rain check. Soon, I promise," she said while walking in her office. Isabella sat back in her office chair and fingered through the arrest and autopsy reports in her client's file. Next, she took a look at the victim's autopsy report and was amazed at her findings:

Subject's name: Annette Simmons
Wt: 132   Ht: 5'7"
D.O.B: 1/16/74   Age: 29
Hair Color: Brown   Eye Color: Brown
Time of Death: 8:00 PM
Cause of Death: 3rd Degree burns and asphyxia
Nature of Occurrence: Arson

Med. Examiner's summary: The subject appears to have died of 3rd degree burns to the body, however, no traces of an accelerant have been found on or near the body. All tests up to this point have been inconclusive. Subject did suffer trauma to the mandibular joint and muscle—three teeth were found at the scene, all of which match the subject's D.N.A. and dental. Toxicology report shows no drug or alcohol use. D.N.A. and fingerprints matching still pending

End of Report

Isabella leaned forward in her chair with her elbows propped on her desk, her hands clasped under her chin as she pondered over what she just read. "Basically, what they're saying is no real physical evidence was found at the scene next to some toothpicks and a bottle of water," she spoke to herself. "In fact, nothing pertaining to this case suggests Mr. Natas had anything to do with the crime. Standing over the body with a bottle of spring water only suggests that he had intentions of putting the fire out."

She'd seen enough. She closed the file and began putting together a motion of dismissal and other pertinent papers to submit at her client's arraignment. Her watch read two minutes after twelve. She'd been busy for about two hours, but it seemed like minutes had passed leaving just under an hour to get to court. She reached for the intercom, picked the switch, and was instantly put in contact with her secretary.

"Listen, Rhonda, if the Denmark Aires' representative calls again, please transfer her to my cell phone and I'll take it from there, okay?"

"Will do, Isabella. And good luck in court."

"Thank you, but I don't need luck, sweetheart, I'm just that good."

"I hear you, girl. Show 'em who's running things around here." They exchanged a few more pleasantries then brought their conversation to a close. Isabella rounded up her client's file along with the motions she put together, then advanced to the door where she was cut off by Kayman as he made his way into her office.

"Hey, kiddo, glad to see you made it in," he said, placing her face in the cups of his hands while rubbing his thumbs around her temple in circular motions. "How's that headache of yours?"

"I'll live. The coffee worked wonders for me," she said, pointing down at an empty Starbucks' container. "Thank you for taking the files out for me and saving me a trip."

"Don't mention it. You would've done the same thing for me, right?"

"Of course, I would—after you reminded me a few times. But hey, as long as it's done, right?" she said meaning it, but not really meaning it at the same time. She cleared her throat. "Anyway, I looked over Mr. Natas' files and I don't see where the D.A. has a case. There's no evidence to build one around."

"Why do you say that?"

"Well for starters, the man wasn't caught committing any wrong doing. Secondly, I see no indication of a resist or struggle between the authorities and my client. And lastly, after they shot him down, the only personal effects on his person were a bottle of spring water and a box of toothpicks. Where's the crime in that?"

"Well, there is an appendix report from a sergeant McCray, that says your client was uttering something that neither he nor his team could make out, not to mention he was holding an obscure object in his hand, two for that mater."

"It was a bottle of Evian Spring Water for Christ's sake!"

"That may well be, but the fact that your client was standing over the deceased body gave probable cause, and the fact that he made a quick move in non-compliance with the sergeant's orders gave justification to their shooting him. However, you are right about one thing—there is no evidence to link him to the fire, so the charges therefore must be thrown out and dismissed due to lack of evidence and violation of the New York police procedural law.

"I see. Thanks, Kayman. I don't know what I'd do without you."

"Shall I name one?"

"Shut up, silly," she said nudging him with her elbow. "Okay, let's be serious now—do you think he killed her? Seriously."

Kayman threw one arm under the other with the top one pointed upward and his finger tapping against his temple as if truly pondering her question. Once satisfied, he turned to her and said matter of factly—seriously, we don't get paid to care if he did or not, our job is to defend our clients to the best of our ability. That's why we make exorbitant figures because, like D.A's, we also use and pull all resources to win a case. Yours, on the other hand, is pretty much set for you."

"That's my point, Kay-Kay." She often called him that when she was pleased with him. "Why did Shuster and Johnson pick me for this case? It's not like I'm special or anything. I can name at least thirty private attorneys that can talk circles around the most aggressive D.A., not to mention make me look less than an amateur."

"Gee, I'd hate to hear you if you didn't have confidence in yourself. Listen, I'm not telling or suggesting you make light of the situation, I just want you to see what Shuster and Johnson sees in you because you deserve it."

She looked at her watch and noticed that fifteen minutes had passed since Kayman entered. "Well, we'll find out how deserving I am in about forty-three minutes. I've got to go, Kayman. I'm already behind schedule and I don't want to be late for the arraignment."

"Okay, but call me as soon as you get in, okay?"

"Done. I promise."

"Good. Now come on and let me walk you to your car."

"Mmm, still persistent on being my knight in shining armor, huh?"

"Every chance I get, but it's going to take more than a sword and shield to beat that dragon with a gravel."

"What are you talking about? What judge?"

Kayman slapped himself upside the head. "Damn, I forgot to tell you—the judge sitting in at the arraignment is Rosenblatt."

"You don't mean Judge Myer Rosenblatt, do you?"

He nodded. Isabella's heart sunk because she knew her task wasn't going to be an easy one, especially not going up against the devil himself. If only she knew who she'd have in her corner.

Three

*M*elsean sat in the corner of a damp, mushy cell in Central Booking, surrounded by society's misfits and undesirables as he awaited arraignment. The doctors were amazed and awe-struck by how fast he recouped from his injuries. Even Melsean himself was amazed to some extent by the miracle of his recovery, but he knew better than to question the works of the higher power. He stared around the cage he occupied with seventy-five other men from primp, neatly dressed individuals in professional attire, to tattered, miserable, and diseased souls that society long forgotten. He peered at his watch—9:58 a.m., he was brought in from the hospital exactly two hours earlier. Sergeant McCray couldn't wait to throw the cuffs on him soon as he heard of his miraculous recovery. You'd think the man had a personal vendetta against him the way he hissed and spit in his face all the way to the squad car.

"I got you, muthafucka. I got you," he declared while leaning his body weight against his healing wounds. He said the infliction of pain was an accident, but Melsean knew better and would hold his grudge until omega.

A young black man stared at Melsean from a distance. His eyes searched him from top to bottom, fascinated with Melsean's taste in style. He was wearing a pair of Jean Gaultier slacks with a matching suit jacket, a black and smoke-gray Coogi turtle neck his receptionist picked out for him at his loft to replace his shot-riddled shirt, and a crisp pair of smoke-gray and black Mauri gators to compliment his getup.

Despite all of that, what really caught the boy's eyes were the platinum chains that adorned Melsean's neck, and he couldn't help but notice how the shade of his garments accentuated the luster of his jewelry. The young man leaned over to his code-fendant, whispering his plans to relinquish Melsean's hold on his jewelry, not knowing that Melsean was aware of him and his cohort's intentions. He watched them through closed eyes as they made their way around sprawled bodies on the floor, trying as hard as possible not to draw attention towards them by moving too fast. They couldn't believe how easy it was going to be to swipe their mark's chains right from under his nose while he wouldn't suspect a thing because he was fast asleep in the corner—or so they thought.

He watched them.

They stopped a few bodies away from him and

started arguing about which was going to take his pricey possessions.

He watched them.

The first one felt he should retrieve them, being it was his plan and idea to involve his buddy in the first place.

He watched them.

The second didn't agree off top, but decided to go along with the initial plan as to not burn bridges with his partner and delay their progress any further. He concluded that after they get and split the profit from the goods, he could start copping his own work and flood the pens with it. However, that would only work if they get out of the jam they're in now. As they neared their victim, he decided to worry about that problem later and concentrate on the task at hand.

Melsean watched in amusement through the undetectable slits of his eyes as the men's obvious thoughts emerged to surface, exposing their greed and desperation to have what was his, but would soon experience hell a hundred times over.

The first man reached Melsean and stood over him, waving his hands about to see if he could rouse his victim. When satisfied that Melsean was truly asleep and oblivious to what was going to take place, he reached down to grab the chains, but was intercepted by Melsean, who grabbed him by the wrist and squeezed with enough pressure to splinter his bones. As he pulled him face-to-face with him and looked deep within his soul, he spotted the fear that inhabited his worthless shell.

"Exodus 20:15, thou shalt not steal," Melsean roared between his teeth, baring two sets of abnormally large canines with no relation to that of humans. "Come closer and stare your future in the eyes and see what my father has in store for you," he said as the space around them became dark. He pulled him closer to the point they were rubbing nose to nose. His victim found himself compelled to stare into the eyes of his oppressor, watching the images that flashed on the dark man's irises. He showed him what he looked like in true form, but concealed himself to the rest who sat or lay throughout the cell, conversing in total oblivion of what was taking place around them. Melsean began to work his mojo, causing his face to take the form of something foreign to anything the young man had ever seen in his life. He stared in horror as he witnessed oblivion in the depth of Melsean's eyes, and his colon and bladder released its contents and soiled his clothes.

"What are you, man?" the young man asked. He pulled away from Melsean and winced in pain from his splintered wrist. "Who are you?"

"Legion, for many demons dwell here," Melsean said, as unknown things writhed beneath the skin of his face, taking on a more hideous appearance as he towered over the young man. Looking back and forth, the young man searched for at least one pair of eyes that bore testimony of the horrid view he had before him; for now he could truly say that he knew death intimately and would soon be dining on retribution for his misguided action in a place as inevitable as death itself, only quicker than expected. The young man closed his eyes and prayed to whatever supreme entity existed beyond his world, time, and space to intervene what he feared would be a slow and painful death (if that's what you would call it) from his tormentor.

Melsean's shadow seemed to triple in size as it covered every man, bench, crack, and corner, turning the entire pen, pitch black as the other occupants remained in their respective places and oblivious to what was taking place. The young man lowered his head in submission as he awaited his imminent ending.

"Danny! Danny!"

The young man opened his eyes to find his co-defendant standing before him, holding him by the shoulders as if to restrain him.

"Let go of me," he snagged himself free from his friend's clutches, trying to get his wind and composure together. "What's wrong with you? You crazy or something?"

"Me? Nah, muthafucka, what's wrong with you? You're the one making a spectacle of yourself and who the fuck is you to be calling somebody crazy anyway? You're the one sitting here crapping on yourself like a two-year old. Anybody got a mirror they can spare so my friend here can see how fucked up he looks?" Danny looked around the pen at the scared, disgusted, confused, and amused faces that watched his alleged performance. He felt something running down his face and legs and out of reflex he wiped at his face with one hand—sticking the other in his pants to discover that it was in fact shit and blood. The mere sight and scent of it made Danny nauseous to the point of frustration, causing him to grab his co-defendant by the throat;

"What did you do to me?"

"I didn't do anything to you," his friend said.

"All right, then what happened to me then?"

"You happened, son. You were supposed to go over there," he pointed at Melsean who was still sleeping peacefully in his corner. "You were supposed to jack the dude for his chains, but somewhere between there and here you just went crazy, partner."

"What the fuck you mean 'crazy'? What exactly did I do?"

"Hmm, let's see, you started out talking something about you shall not steal, then out of the blue, you started punching yourself in the face. I ain't gonna front, that was some funny shit at first, but then you kept beating and beating yourself till I thought you were going to kill yourself. That's when I came over and got you out of it."

As Danny's co-defendant explained to him his actions, he found himself hit with the realization that what he saw, or at least what he thought he saw, was real. He tried to avoid the inevitable, but in the end, found himself compelled to turn and gaze at Melsean, who was still lying in the same place he was since he got there. Danny stared in fear knowing that he was the only one in their pen, or any pen for that matter, that witnessed the face of the greater evil than any one of them could fathom.

No more than a minute later, a count officer showed up at the cell door.

"Natas? Mr. Melsean Natas, come on. It's show time. The judge would like to see you now."

Melsean showed no signs of worry as he allowed himself to be released and escorted, along with another inmate to the courtroom, but before them and the officer left, he turned to face the man, and tapped his finger against his temple and silently spoke.

"Remember what I said, because I'll be watching you." With that, he walked away, leaving Danny's co-defendant and fellow pen-mates confused by the silent exchange that took place causing Danny's co-defendant to inquire.

"Yo, what was that all about? Did I miss something here?"

Danny didn't respond to his friend, instead he just stood in a state of shock because he knew exactly what Melsean meant as he exited down the corridor. He could still feel the chill of his presence. He was glad the officer came and took the stranger when he did, but he knew that he hadn't seen the last of his eternal tormentor, and just the mere thought of what he would do to him the next time they met caused Danny to defecate on himself again, emptying the contents of his bowels inside his jeans as the sound of disgruntled criminals expressing their disgust at Danny's lack of control could be heard all the way down the corridor.

Four

In the matter of People versus Melsean Natas, Indictment number 0666/04, case presiding by Honorable Judge Myer Rosenblatt, will the defense and prosecution please stand and state your name and title for the record?" the court clerk instructed. He handed Melsean's case file to the judge as Melsean stared blankly past the podium in which the judge's bench and witness stand were located as if he wasn't the least bit interested in the proceedings.

The prosecutor for the state rose and addressed the court.

"Good afternoon, Your Honor. Desiree Wilson for the Kings County prosecution's office, and I'll be presenting the case in the interest of the people, Your Honor."

The judge nodded in agreement with the D.A.'s intentions. "Very well then—and to the defense?"

"Yes, Your honor. Isabella Danpier, Esquire for the

Jacob, Finkelstein and Phillips law firm in Long Island, and I will be handling the defendant's case, Your Honor."

"Good," the judge said, focusing his attention back on the D.A.. "Will the prosecution please read the charges?"

"Yes, Your Honor. The defendant, Melsean Natas, was charged early this month with one count of murder in the first degree, as defined in the statutes, under Penal Law: § 150.20, subdivisions (A), (B), (C), and (I). He cold-bloodedly killed his alleged girlfriend, one Ms. Annette Simmons, on the night of June fifteenth, setting her aflame after giving her a couple of hard blows to her face, causing her to suffer trauma to the head.

The Sussex County Medical Examiner also indicated numerous lacerations around the mandibular joints on either side, and one under the victim's right eye. The people are asking Your Honor to deny bail to the defendant. His actions were anything but humane and should be treated with the same courtesy he showed the victim—none!" The D.A. returned to her seat, crossed her legs, then looked to her right and stared at Melsean with disgust as she fingered through her folder for additional notes pertaining to the case.

Isabella glanced sideways out of the corner of her eye at Melsean, in attempt to get an idea of the kind of person he was. She admired his 6'2" frame, broad shoulders, and exceptionally small feet for someone his size and build. His hazel eyes seemed to compliment his attire. It seemed as though when one looked at his face from the left, he appeared to be passive, but the opposite side contradicted his look, exposing a more rogue expression.

The stenographer stared back and forth between Isabella and the judge with her fingers poised at the keys on her stenograph eagerly awaiting the next sound, syllable, word, or sentence to be recorded. Judge Rosenblatt broke the silence, turning his attention to Isabella.

"Would the defense like to state their case for the record?"

"Yes, Your Honor," Isabella said rising out of her chair, approaching the judge's bench. "Your Honor, my client, Mr. Natas, has done nothing wrong here. If anybody's the blame, it would most certainly be N.Y.P.D. for their duplicitous actions not to mention premature judgment against my client..." she pointed at Melsean, "who was repeatedly shot by a Lionel McDermond of N.Y.'s Special Riots Division, when he possessed no weapon or immediate threat to them. More so, I move to motion that the said charges be dismissed against my client due to lack of evidence and violation of my client, Mr. Natas', constitutional rights to due process and timely access to appear before the grand jury as described in diction 130.30. However, I ask Your Honor to grant my client bail until a hearing can be made and allocated and my client exonerated of all charges, Your Honor, thank you."

With that said, Isabella returned to her seat beside Melsean and awaited Judge Rosenblatt's decision. There was no doubt in her mind that the outcome of this hearing could go either way. She stared for a moment at the judge as she read through Melsean's case file and assessed what both counsels had brought to the bench. She then turned to her left and watched as the prosecutor sat in slouch posture, twiddling her fingers, anxiously awaiting the judge's decision. Isabella then directed her eyes to her right and focused her attention on Melsean, who to this point still remained indifferent by the charges he faced. She wasn't sure what to say or do to break the ice of silence between her and her client being they never spoke a word to each other, but she knew in order to help him, she'd have to build some kind of rapport with him. So without thinking, she patted him on the thigh just above the knee.

"Don't worry. I think we have him right where we want him." For the first time since they've seen each other, Melsean spoke in the most eloquent and nonchalant voice Isabella had ever heard.

"I'm not worried or troubled by any of this. What I am is puzzled because I was shot for trying to put out the flame that consumed my friend."

His eyes seemed to weigh down on Isabella's body as he stared in unbroken concentration, penetrating her clothes, and resting them on her naked flesh. She couldn't explain her feeling of euphoria, as hundreds of small, invisible hands explored every concave of her body until they made their way down to her half-hidden gumdrop of flesh between her legs and replaced its warm hands for wet tongues. She tried to resist their welcoming embrace to her sensitivity, but to no avail; she only hoped that what was happening to her was not being witnessed by the other court attendants who at this time seemed oblivious to her experience.

Isabella envisioned Melsean reaching out to her, placing his hands around the small of her back and raising her up on the table as he planted himself between her thighs. He then gently cupped her breast while rubbing his thumbs in circular motion around her areolas causing Isabella to respond to this stimulation. All the while, Melsean kept whispering the command *"Tell me what you want and I'll give it to you"* over and over until the words remained securely locked away in her subconscious

"Ms. Danpier? Ms. Danpier?"

Isabella heard her name being called from a distance, but became more distant the closer it got, pulling her from her fugue state.

"Ms. Danpier!"

She snapped her head up and focused on the judge. "Yes, Your Honor?"

"It's nice to have you back with us. I hope the court isn't keeping you away from more important matters," he said in a condescending manner.

"No, Your Honor. I was just putting my papers together and got a little sidetracked, that's all."

"Very well. How about answering my question, that is if you don't mind?"

"I'm sorry, Your Honor?"

He sighed. "Do you have anything to add and make known to the court before I respond?"

"No, Your Honor. The defense trusts that Your Honor will rule justly in favor and respect to what's in the best interest of justice. Thank you." Isabella sat back in her chair, exhaled deeply, and turned to look at Melsean, who seemed not to have moved an inch since the proceedings started. However, there was a difference in his facial expression for now he was lightly smirking.

The judge took this time to render his verdict.

"After going over the records and hearing both sides from the people and defense, I find it hard to ignore the severity of this kind of case. I feel it would be callous of me to dismiss the charges without seeing where the people are going with their argument."

"Your Honor?" Isabella pleaded.

"Silence, Ms. Danpier. You were given every opportunity to give your say on this matter, as the district attorney, but now it is my turn, and I intend to render my decision uninterrupted by either of you, agreed?"

"Yes, Your Honor," the two attorneys said in sequence.

"Marvelous. Now where was I? Oh yes, I want to see where the prosecutor is going with her case, so the defendant's motion for dismissal is hereby denied."

"Desiree turned in her chair until she was face-to-face with Isabella and began to grin snidely, silently wording, "Who's the champ this time?"

Isabella fumed, but was taken aback by Melsean's hand gently patting hers in a gesture to be easy and let the judge continue.

The judge took off his glasses and rubbed his

eyes, and returned them back to their proper place and continued stating his decision. "However, my denial is only to the limit that I am going to leave it to the grand jury to decide if there's any relevancy to this case worth pursuing. As far as bail is concerned, I feel it is best for the defendant to remain in the custody of the Department of Corrections based on the information before me."

Isabella was about to object again, but Melsean once more patted her hand, this time adding a little squeeze to it causing her to calm down and let fate take its course.

The judge continued. "Of course, the courts must take in consideration the defendant's past criminal history, community ties, and contributions as a matter of law. Based on what I've read in his record, I have no choice but to release the defendant on his own recognizance."

The prosecutor rose out of her chair, stupefied by what she just heard. She wanted to object, but something stole her voice and held it at bay.

Melsean leaned over and whispered something in Isabella's ear and Isabella addressed the court.

"Your Honor, my client has brought it to my attention that due to him being shot, hospitalized, and incarcerated, he was kicked out of his apartment and lost all of his possessions. The only other place of residence my client has was the address of the deceased. Can the courts please assist in finding a temporary, if not permanent, address for the defendant until he can establish himself?"

Judge Rosenblatt looked at her considerately

and replied, "Yes, I have the perfect place for your client—with you," he pointed at her.

"With me? Your Honor, surely you can't be—"

"Serious?" he cut in. "I can't be more serious. After all, counselor, he is your client and counsels have an obligation to their client's welfare when looked at from a professional standpoint. So with that said, this case is adjourned until next Wednesday for grand jury."

"Your Honor, can we…"

"No we cannot! This case is adjourned, I said. My suggestion to you is that you take this time to go and take your client home to get settled in and work on your client's story for the grand jury." He beat his gavel against the bench, got up, and walked away leaving Isabella alone in the company of Melsean.

"Well, I guess it's to my house then," she said, placing her files back in her briefcase.

Melsean turned towards her in a casual manner and flatly spoke. "You don't have to do this. I can get a room in a hotel and I'm sure the company I work for will foot the bill."

At first, Isabella contemplated accepting his giving her a way out, but in his eyes, she couldn't quite put her finger on it, something just seemed to be against her less than hospitable thoughts. "No, Mr. Natas, you're coming with me. You heard the judge; we counselors have an obligation to our clients. Besides, the money I'm getting paid to defend you well over compensates for my forced hospitality," she said jokingly.

"Well, at least let me buy you lunch as a way of showing my appreciation. What do you say?"

How can I say no to a man with eyes like yours? she thought. "Sure. I'd like that."

"Good. Come on, let's get out of here. I'm starting to feel the walls close in on me."

"Oh, you're claustrophobic?"

"No. Law-phobic," he said, rubbing his wrists where the handcuffs had earlier been and left light impressions of their past presence.

Isabella laughed. "All right, let's get out of here."

They walked out of the court room leaving Melsean's shadow behind in his seat, staring at the two as they made their way down the hall to the elevator.

Five

*I*sabella and Melsean sat comfortably in the back of Brooklyn's number one Chinese restaurant, Kum Kaus, located on Myrtle Avenue in Clinton Hills; enjoying two house specialties of Melsean's choice. Neither of the two said much during the trip there, nor as they sat waiting for their orders to arrive. Isabella stared blankly at the basket of fortune cookies between her and Melsean. Unsure of how to break the silence between them, she decided the direct approach would be the most feasible.

"So, do you come here often?"

"When time permits," Melsean said, training his hazel eyes on her. "I'm busy more often than not. If I'm not on my job, I'm at the gym."

"I can tell," she said staring at his protruding physique, feeling a slight touch of embarrassment for her lack of good shape. "Look at you. I suspected you were a personal trainer when I first saw you."

"Really? But we both know you're not because

the company you work for paid me handsomely to see to it that you walk."

"Elementary, my dear Watson," he said imitating Sherlock Holmes. "Since we're playing the honesty game, I guess it would be rude of me not to reciprocate. I have to admit that you are a very attractive woman."

"Really? I don't recall you once looking at me during your arraignment."

"Who says you have to look directly at a person in order to see them? It is said in the Bible that no man could look directly upon God lest they should die."

"Oh, and what is that supposed to mean?"

He leaned forward, averting his eyes away from her, but bringing his lips within kissing range. Isabella's pulse quickened as she anticipated Melsean's advances, lingering on the fact that only the thin layer of air stood between them. Both of their breaths intermingled together forming an unseen union, but was just as quickly broken when he moved his lips to her ear.

"You are heavenly," he said, and returned back to his original sitting posture.

Isabella resented the way his words got her all hot and bothered. Never in her twenty-six years of living has a man stirred her emotions as Melsean did, but what's worse is she's only known him for less than five hours and already finding the man irresistible. She realized her only escape from her lust was to focus her attention on business and leave the personal alone until she can get a better handle on her emotions.

"Huh hmm..." she cleared her throat, "anyway, let's discuss what happened on the night of your girlfriend's death."

"I didn't do it!" he snapped as he opened and closed his fists. His reaction shocked Isabella. It was like he had two personalities harboring the same space. Even as his face contorted to show his anger toward the subject, his eyes remained calm, collected, and innocent.

"Listen, you need to calm down. Next week you have to appear before the grand jury and should expect the questions I ask to be raised."

His face softened. "You're right, I apologize, Mrs. Danpier. I didn't mean..."

She fanned off his apology. "First of all, I'm single. So lay off the 'Mrs.' Crap. Secondly, I prefer to be called Isabella. And last, I accept and appreciate your apology, but it wasn't necessary. I'm quite sure that I would have reacted the same way had our roles been reversed. However, the reality is that we both have a problem here, so I need you to help me help you out of your situation. Agreed?"

"Agreed."

"Good. Now where the hell is our food?"

"Relax, Isabella. The orders I placed for us isn't an easy dish. It has to be perfect...like other things," he said, boring his eyes into her naked soul. Isabella wasn't used to feeling the way Melsean caused her to feel. His words alone caused a warm sensation to overtake her body as invisible hands worked their way between her legs, prying them apart, and allowing the warm air to lap at her sensitivity. In her ear she heard the same voice she heard in the court-room, taunting her sexually frustrated body.

Tell me what you want and I'll give it to you.

She felt herself drifting until a familiar voice began to call her name from afar, making its way closer as it pulled her out of her trance.

"Isabella? Are you okay? I was telling you about the special dish I had in store for you and you were telling me how you looked forward to it, that's when your voice trailed off. I thought you were play-ing at first, but once you started making faces, I knew something had to be wrong."

"What faces?" she asked stunned by his shocking revelation.

"You honestly don't know, do you?" He leaned forward in his chair, holding a silk handkerchief and wiped the beads of sweat off of her face and returned it to his pocket. "Your eyes were in a trance and your face appeared to be flushed."

She traced her hands across her face then attempted to get up, but Melsean reached for her arm and gently prodded her to remain seated. "No, don't try to get up. You're parched, let's get you something to drink and then we can go because you don't look so hot."

"Thanks for pointing that out," she said with a note of sarcasm.

"You know what I mean," he said while signal-ing for the waiter's attention, and then spoke in Chinese dialect as the waiter nodded in approval and hurried off.

"What did you say to him?"

"I said, me and the young lady have changed our minds about the meal. I told him you are not feeling well, so could he bring you a bottle of club soda and bring me the check."

"You didn't say all of that."

"In the Chinese language, they don't have as many characters as in the English language, so it doesn't require as much dialogue."

"I'd never imagine that you would know Chinese."

"I know six other languages. I was what you would call a marine brat. My father was a corporal spokesman that mediated all of Americas' dealings with foreign lands, so I pretty much was taught everything he knew."

"Ahh, an officer and a gentleman type, I like that."

"More like a thug and a righteous hustler, or at least that's how my father perceived me. Every chance I got, I would sneak off the base and get my grind on."

"Oh, and just what kind of grinding were you doing?"

"Sorry counselor, but I believe I'm going to have to plead the fifth on that."

"Come on, Melsean, you can tell me. Remember attorney-client confidentiality, does that ring a bell?"

"Yeah, so does Strickland verses Washington, so it's best to let sleeping dogs lie."

"You certainly know how to kill the mood,

don't you?"

"It's a gift," he said dismissingly. "But never mind that, let's focus on getting you home because you don't look so well. First, I suggest you take a few swallows of club soda. That should settle your stomach and I'll drive."

Just as he finished his sentence, the Chinese waiter approached the table passing Isabella a glass of fizzing water and Melsean the bill, which he paid on the spot with his platinum card. After Isabella had finished her water, and the waiter returned his card to him, he thanked the man in Chinese and signaled Isabella that it was time to go. She immediately got up and began to follow him until they were side-by-side, then decided to break the silence between them.

"I'm not done with the questioning. As soon as I'm feeling better, we are going to continue where we left off."

Melsean turned to make eye contact with her. He couldn't believe how vulnerable she looked right now, especially after seeing the feistier spitfire side of her in court. Nevertheless, he knew better than to make light of her demands.

"I look forward to it."

"Good," she passed him the keys. "Let's go home."

"Okay, but where is home?"

"Don't worry, I'll navigate."

"Aye, aye, captain. We best be shoving off then," he said imitating pirate lingo.

"Umm, I love a man of danger, but what's the

deal with the silk handkerchief?"

"What's the deal with you catching an orgasm in a crowded restaurant—a Chinese one at that?"

"Who said I had or was having an orgasm?" she blushed. "I didn't have an orgasm, Melsean."

"No?"

"No, I almost had an orgasm. There's a difference."

"Yes, I suppose you're right. After all, it's not every day that you see an aspiring attorney get flushed in public," he lightly elbowed her on the arm as they exited the restaurant.

The ride to her house was a quiet one next to Isabella giving directions every now and then. For the most part, she just looked out the window in a world of her own.

From Melsean's view, she was a very attractive woman. She was yellow-boned with light brown eyes that reflected the rays of the sun whenever they came in contact. He wanted to run his fingers through her sandy-brown hair, but thought against it, knowing to do so would violate all ethics of business. He withdrew his hand, placing it back on the steering wheel, and focused his attention on the road.

Almost an hour later, they were pulling into the driveway of a gated community in East Hampton. It was a beautiful Villa like the ones you'd see in the Bay Hill area of Florida with a walk around front porch. It was beautifully painted in white with trims of pink to radiate her femininity. Both sides of the house showed views of trees with about a quarter-acre of open space containing a closed-in pool, outside kitchen, complete with an island and gas grill and stove.

"You have a beautiful home, Isabella. I'm impressed."

"Oh yeah?" she said wiping her eyes. "Wait until you see the inside. Come on, I'll show you."

She wasn't lying. Upon entering the house, Melsean immediately fell in love with its homely appearance. She had four large rooms, three of which were unoccupied, three and a half bathrooms, and windows that overlooked a beautifully land-scaped patio with fountains and flowers. Each room in the house offered its own distinct story. The kitchen was covered with textiles, the dining room, hallway, and bedrooms had hard wood floors, and each bathroom possessed marble floors. In the living room there was a sixty-two-inch, flat-screen TV with a dual DVD player connected to it. However, what really got his attention was her kitchen. She had a wide selection of fresh fruits and vegetables; she had a fully stocked cupboard and refrigerator that indicated that she did her own cooking.

"You mean to tell me you live her all by your-self?"

"Yes, is that so hard to believe?"

"Nah, I'm not saying that. I just never seen a kitchen as stocked as yours—especially not for just one person."

"Well, you never know when a judge is going to stick one of your clients on you, so it's best to be prepared."

"I see you're not going to let that go, huh? Listen, I'm just as uncomfortable as you are with these living arrangements, but I am willing to adjust provided that you are also willing." He looked down at his watch. "Listen, I have to be somewhere, so it's best that I leave now."

"No, you don't have to go. I was just playing around. If it was something I said then..."

"No, Isabella, I wasn't offended by what you said. It just so happens that I have an appointment with a friend and I can't be late."

"Oh, and who might this friend be?"

"I really can't say because it's personal, but what I can tell you is that it's important, so can I please borrow your car for a couple of hours and I promise to return it in one piece."

"Sure," she tossed him the keys. "Go handle your business and I'm going to take a shower and get a few z's. We can finish our discussion when you get back, agreed?"

"Fine. Is this the part where we're supposed to kiss and say our good-byes?"

"No, this is where you do you Charlie Chaplin routine and shuffle your ass out the door before I decide to take my keys back."

"All right, I get your point. I'm gone." He opened the door, looking back only once, and closed the door behind him.

Isabella dropped onto her plush couch and sighed. She couldn't believe how incredibly gorgeous her client was, however, she wasn't too fond of the high school crush sensation she was going through,

either. Melsean's presence alone caused her hormones to go into overdrive.

"This is insane," she said pushing up from the
couch and making her way to the bathroom. She
walked inside the shower and immediately turned on
the water for her bath, adjusting it to her liking.
Next, she opened her medicine cabinet, reached in
and pulled out a packet of aromatherapy bath salt
and poured it into the filling tub. She then immediately began disrobing until the only thing that covered her was a thin patch of sandy brown hair that
covered her pubic area.

Before settling in the tub, she lit her aromatherapy candles on each corner of the tub, creating a force field of a fresh scent, and she allowed the
heated fragrant water to work the kinks out of her
body. Five minutes later she was fast asleep and
thinking about Melsean.

Six

S*argent* Matthew McCray sat with his feet propped up in a La-Z-Boy chair with four empty bottles out of a six pack of ice cold Guinness Stout beside him on a glass stand. He was watching game three of the finals between the Detroit Pistons and the Indiana Pacers. Detroit was up twelve points, which didn't please him much, especially since he had seven big ones on Indiana, and it wasn't looking good.

"Dammit, Reggie, follow through with your shot!" he yelled at the TV screen. "Pick and roll! Come on, Jermaine! We still got time on the clock, lay off the fast breaks!" He felt good knowing his wife went over to her mother's for the week. She didn't approve of his excessive drinking, nor was she a big fan of basketball.

Matt hasn't been sleeping as peacefully as before, since that arson case with that quack nature, gnat-up-the-ass, or whatever his name was. The image of that poor girl's burned body still remained stained in his subconscious and tortured him when the night chases the last hint of daylight from the sky. He could still remember the look on the man's face as he loomed over the human heap of char like some kind of sac religions ritual or something. The thing that troubled him about this case was how somebody could burn a body with a bottle of spring water and a box of toothpicks. Probably a question that will never be answered unless he sought them from the only man that could answer it, and he could never bring himself to do that without the uncontrollable urge to beat the man's face in with the butt of his gun and a 16 band receiver.

"I hope they crucify you, you sick son of a bitch!" he said out loud. "What the fuck am I so unhappy for, we got that motherfucker. For what he's done, the judge is guaranteed to see to it that he winds up at the end of a hundred-thousand volt chair." He focused his attention back to the screen just in time to see Jermaine O'Neal give Ron Artest an alley-oop, when all of a sudden the screen went snowy. "What the fuck? Come on, not right now! Don't do this to me!" He rose and walked over to the television and played with the wireless digital antenna until the game came back on.

"Don't fuck with me," he said pointing accusingly at the screen. "Fuck up on your time, not on mine." He turned away from the screen and walked back over to his seat. As soon as he sat and propped his feet up, the screen went snowy again. "Son-of-a-bitch. What the fuck is going on here?" he asked, lowering the footrest again and rising from the seat.

He walked over to the TV and was about to play with the antenna when the game came back on the screen, exposing Ben Wallace scoring his sixteenth point. "Shit! What the fuck do I have to do to make a dollar here, huh? I can't win for losing."

He turned around and was about to return to his chair when the television screen went blank as if the fuse blew. "What the hell?" He pressed the power switch to no avail. Whatever energy was in there was long gone now. He looked behind the television and noticed that the cord wasn't plugged in the outlet, and worst of all, the television cord was missing from the television. Matthew became nervous, reaching down to his waist to see if he had his service weapon on him and felt relieved when he felt the bulge of his Sig Saur P228 pressing against his pelvic bone. While reaching into his waist band, the phone rang causing Matthew to pull out his gun, at the same time spinning on his right pivot and training his weapon on the phone. He took a deep breath, let it out, and walked over to the phone and picked it up, "Hello?"

A monstrous voice answered on the other line in a low, whispering fashion,

"Vengeance is mine sayeth the lord."

Melsean kissed Isabella gently on the back of her neck as she sat between his legs in her bathtub. He reached his arms around her and took hold of her breasts and ran his index finger in circular motion around her areolas while giving her nipples a light tweaking every so often. Isabella could feel Melsean's man tool pressing against the small of her back, desperate to penetrate something. She lifted up to allow his shaft to slide between the crack of her ass, causing Melsean to groan in frustration until he couldn't take it anymore. He reached under her legs, picked her up, and slowly sat her onto his manhood. Isabella liked being dominated. She was by far no masochist, but welcomed the intensity of his every thrust. Melsean gripped her thighs and began to give her stronger and more direct strokes as if he was trying to fit his balls inside of her.

Isabella closed her eyes and cried out, but begged him for more as she felt her orgasm nearing. "Harder, faster," she gasped, biting down on her lower lip, drawing a trickle of blood, as she reached climax. Isabella collapsed atop of Melsean as her body went through the last of its sexual convulsions. This had been one of the strongest orgasms she'd had in her life. Never before had her inner walls felt like an actual fist clenching and relaxing; every contraction beat urgently against her pelvic bone causing her to wince at the pain, yet revel in the pleasure of it.

"You fuck like a wild animal," she said, opening her eyes to focus on Melsean, but he wasn't there—only a hideous looking thing with small spike-like objects coming out of its face and one-inch fangs on the top and bottom of his mouth. Its ears had the same black, leathery substance like bats. The body was identical to Melsean's just with a different face—and boy did that make a difference. He looked her directly in the face and responded to her comment with a snarl.

"What can I say, you brought the beast out of me," he said while raking his talon fingers across her breasts causing Isabella to jerk out of her sleep screaming and holding her breast. It took almost a minute for her to realize that it was just a bad dream. The water in the tub had become uncomfortably cold and she could hear the doorbell ringing. She jumped out of the tub, put on a terrycloth robe, and went to see who was at the door.

She looked through the peephole, gave off a sigh, and opened the door. Her friend April came in carrying a healthy size casserole dish of peach cobbler, and judging by the oven mitts she was wearing and light smoke patches, she could tell that she had just finished making it.

"April, please tell me you didn't disturb my bath so you can bring me a cobbler that hasn't even cooled off yet."

"Actually, it wasn't for you—technically it is, but actually it isn't."

"What's that supposed to mean? If it isn't for me then who is—wait a minute," she thought about it for a second. "You didn't make this for my guest, did you?"

"Girl, you know I like to show southern hospitality to potential friends. Especially when a good friend of mine hasn't been on a date since...well, let's just say you haven't been on a date in a while."

"Listen, are you going to stand there all day or are you going to put that cobbler in the kitchen? I know it's burning your hand, and you're over here rain dancing on my floor. Go put it down, silly."

April walked past Isabella, hurrying toward the kitchen. Isabella couldn't help but smile to herself thinking back to how she met April.

❦

April came from a small town in North Carolina called Bath. This town was only about a couple miles long, so you can imagine how close their community was. She went to school in Roper until the age of thirteen, and switched to junior high in Belhaven. She was very pretty with her huge, brown eyes, high cheekbones, and healthy frame. All the guys in her town competed daily to win the attention of April, but she was never interested. It wasn't until a guy named Ramir came down from New York to hustle that April decided to submit to the advances of a man. Everyday, Ramir would come around to April's house and get his rap on, splurging money every chance he got. He'd stay for a week and then leave for three, always returning on time and spending a good part of it with her. Three months of courting resulted in her getting pregnant with his child, and she decided at Ramir's request to move to New York with him.

He was the perfect gentleman up until the last two months of her pregnancy. By mistake she stumbled across a pair of thongs and she knew they weren't hers—good girls didn't wear panties like those—or at least that was what she was taught. When she tried to confront Ramir about it, he chose not to speak out loud, but responded in domestic Morse code, which included beating the words on every available area of her body. Her brain didn't register the first couple of hits. It wasn't until his fist came crashing against her ribs that she decided to block, or at least attempt to ward off his blows until he calm down and afford her the opportunity to escape. That didn't happen; he mercilessly beat his fist onto her belly causing her to go into premature labor.

Ramir panicked, but still managed to hold himself enough to call the paramedics. While waiting, he began rehearsing the concocted story they would tell the paramedics to explain April's injuries. Of course, that wasn't the case when they finally arrived—they knew exactly what caused her injuries and immediately requested that the N.Y.P.D meet them at the Lutheran's Medical Center. Two things happened that day, one good, one bad—the bad thing was April's child was a still born due to massive trauma; the good news was that Ramir was charged with attempted murder, assault, reckless endanger-ment, and infanticide, and will not be getting out of prison for a very long time.

At that time, Isabella was just starting out in her law career in civil practice and had to do a lot of pro bono cases. She was assigned to handle April's suit against Ramir who had a very large nest egg in various banks. Due to him moving her so far away from any family relatives, his recent action against her, her lack of adequate education, and basically no means to support herself, the court granted her eighty-five percent of everything he owned, including possession of his recently purchased house. Since that day, April and Isabella have been the closest of friends next to Kayman, and even moved into the same villa-house in Pennsylvania.

⚜

April returned to the living room eating one of the sticky buns that Isabella had bought from Cinn-a-buns. She took a seat opposite Isabella, resting her right leg under her.

"So, tell me all about your new friend," April said in between bites of her sticky bun.

"First of all, he is not a friend, he is a client," Isabella said defensively.

"Really? So, what's your client doing at his attorney's house, huh?"

"It's complicated."

"Humor me."

"All right. My client is suspected of murdering his girlfriend."

"Ouch!"

"Yeah, I thought the same thing when Kayman told me about it. Anyway, the presiding judge granted my client bail on R-on-R."

"Okay, pause," she threw her hands in a stop sign fashion. "Does your client have a name and what the fuck is an R and R?"

"Oh, sorry. His name is Melsean Natas, and it's not R and R, goofball, it's R-on-R, meaning Released on own Recognizance."

April looked at her puzzled. Isabella sucked her

teeth exasperated. "It means released on your word to come back, you know, like a documented promise. Now shut up and let me finish the story." She cleared her throat. "Now where was I? Oh yeah, so Melsean was telling me about how he got incarcerated and lost his apartment. I brought it to the judge's attention and he decided to make me in charge of my client until suitable living arrangements can be made for him."

April didn't say anything—which was a first for her. She just stared at Isabella in disbelief. After thirty seconds of silence, Isabella decided to prod something out of her friend.

"Well, don't you have anything to say?"

April blinked her eyes a few times, shaking her head, and responded. "Yeah, I do. You're a lucky bitch, Issey."

"What do you mean lucky? There's nothing lucky about what's going on here."

"Like hell it isn't. It's like the judge can sense that you're in need of a good scraping, so he dropped dick at your front door."

They both laughed.

"So, where is your rent-a-dick, huh?"

"I don't know. He just said he had something personal to take care of."

"Sounds to me like somebody went out to tie up the loose ends on whatever he was into."

"All right, that's enough. It's time for you to go, April."

"What? What did I say?"

"What you shouldn't have, that's for sure."

"Come on, girl. Admit it; the guy's a cutie, right or wrong?"

"Okay, he's cute. What's your point?"

"My point is when I saw ya'll get out of the car and walk up to your door, you two looked like the perfect pair—you know, y'all just naturally fit together.

Isabella considered what her friend was telling her. She most certainly found Melsean attractive, but that goes against all professional ethics and she wasn't going to risk her career for a cute face and possible great lay.

"Listen, I'm a bit tired right now, April, so come back later and we'll talk." She got up and escorted April to the door.

"Okay, love, I can take a hint, but I'll be back later," she said walking out the door.

"I'll see you later then." Isabella closed the door behind her. She hated getting rid of April like that, but right now all she could do was wonder where Melsean was and why he was so hush-hush about it. Other than that, the nightmare she had before April came troubled her. She had a gut feeling inside that something bad was going to happen very soon.

Seven

"**Who** is this?" Sergeant Matthew screamed into the phone as he attempted to put a face with the voice on the other end of the line, but found it to be a fruitless task. His only hope was to find out what the person wanted from him and track him down. He had recently bought a compact tracking device from spy.com. It was a little box with a screen that pinpoints the exact geographic area of the caller. Matthew's phone also came with caller ID, so he pressed the display button to see who his mystery prank caller was. Seven numbers flashed on the screen revealing an all too familiar number—his own.

"No fucking way," he said, scouring every corner of his living room. Common sense told him that wherever your wired phone is, the perp was sure to be close by, so that meant he had to be in his bedroom or bathroom. Sergeant Matthew began scaling the walls with his pistol stretched before him in the traditional combat stance. He came to his bedroom door and found it half closed. This struck him as odd because he never closes the door, nor has he had a reason to. With his free hand, he lightly opened the door, training his gun on every potential hiding place. His instincts told him to check places he would less likely be in, but the cop in him went against his better judgment.

Turn on the lights stupid, his instincts told him. He flicked the switch for the bedroom light, but nothing happened. Then it occurred to him that maybe a fuse blew, but that wouldn't explain the ripped-out television cord. *Look up.* He looked up and saw something that made the hair on the back of his neck stand straight up—someone or something had busted the light bulb and damn near ripped all the wires out of the ceiling. What troubled Matthew more about this was he couldn't recall hearing any noises and he'd been home all day, today. His gut feeling was telling him he could back out of this room, run for the door, and never look back, but the cop in him wanted to stay and find the cocksucker, and make him wish he never picked this place to ambush.

"Whoever you are, I know you're in here. I don't know what you want, or how you got in here for that matter, but I'm a cop and I don't think you want this to go down the way it's about to if you don't come out now!" Sweat trickled down his cheeks as he scanned the room inch by inch, checking behind the doors, closets, pushing clothes to the side, and using his foot to sweep the closet's floor in case someone was hiding down there. Everywhere he looked turned up with nothing. He even went and checked the bathroom, kitchen, cabinets, cupboards, and closets, finding only what belonged in there all in their respective places. He returned to his bedroom and sat trying to figure out if there was something he was forgetting. As far as he was concerned, there were no other places a man could hide. He stood up and started to laugh for being so paranoid.

"You're a piece of work, Sergeant McCray," he said to himself, and he was about to go check the fuse box when his cell phone rang in his pocket. He took it out and checked the caller ID and found again that it was his home phone number dialing him, but that phone never left his bedroom. He turned around and looked toward his nightstand, but nothing was there. He was about to back out of the room when all of a sudden something reached from under the bed and grabbed his ankles with it's clawed hands and pulled him full force into the side of the bed, shattering both shinbones.

In reflex, Sergeant McCray fired off six shots directly at the part of the bed where the hands were coming from. Four of the shots hit their mark causing the sharp-clawed beast to release him. At first, Matthew's mind didn't register his injuries, so he attempted to run, but instead he feebly collapsed to the floor. Just as fast as he fell did the beast slide from under the opposite side of the bed, heading directly for Sergeant McCray. Out of fear and desperation, Matthew aimed his weapon in the direction of the shadowy figure, but was instantly kicked in the temple before he could get off another shot and was forced into an unconscious state.

For what felt like hours, Matthew found himself floating in a dark void. He couldn't see, hear, touch, taste, or smell anything. Nothing mattered in this abysmal place, nor did he care. His only concern was escaping the madness that brought him there in the first place. Out of nowhere, an intense rush of pain came flooding through his body, forcing him back to a reality and fate to grim too fathom. He awoke screaming, but not on the floor as he had last been, but rather against the wall with his clothes meticulously nailed to it. His arms were spread apart while his knees were slightly bent and nailed to the wall causing his feet to rest flatly against it.

"Who are you? What are you doing to me?"

The shadow in the left corner of the room began to come towards him. "I haven't done anything to you yet," the shadowed figure said, humored by the scent of fear seeping out of the pores of the man.

"Wait a minute," Sergeant McCray said, trying to see through the darkness. "I know that voice— you're that sick fuck that killed your girlfriend a few weeks ago—yeah, that was you all right. You set the poor woman on fire, you crazy son-of-a-bitch."

"You really should watch the profanity. It's not good to speak such abominations, especially when you don't know the person."

"Oh, I know you enough, dammit—enough to

know they should lock you up and throw away the key."

"Funny. Before you said 'I hope they crucify you, you sick son-of-a-bitch,'" he mimicked Matthew's voice. "You know I admire you, Matthew, you don't mind if I call you Matthew, do you?"

"It's Sergeant McCray to you, you sadistic cocksucker. Why don't you step out of the shadows and face me like a man?"

"Okay, Matthew, I'll come out," Melsean said, stepping out of the shadows to reveal a face far more horrid than anything Sergeant McCray could ever concoct in his imagination. He hung from the wall pissing on himself as Melsean finished his sentence.

"But I assure you, I am no man."

"You're not what I saw that night," Sergeant McCray cried, wishing he could kill himself and avoid whatever the beast before him had in store for him.

"How can you be sure who or what you saw that night? Had it been all the gun smoke from your shooting me that impaired your sight and perception? Did the gun smoke make you unaware of your inevitable fate? Don't get me wrong, I appreciate a man that knows what he wants and is not afraid to die for or because of it. Christ felt the same way as you do—in fact, you remind me a great deal of Christ, and it's for that reason that I must insure that you receive nothing less of his ending grace."

"What do you mean?"

"Come on, you're a wise man—all right, let's put it this way, I am going to make sure that you share the same experience that Christ did in his last hours," Melsean said reaching for the empty Guinness stout bottles on the table. "So, I've decided to crucify you."

Sergeant McCray, sensing the coming of an early demise, attempted one last time to break free, jerking himself side to side to tear away from the nails in the wall. Out of nowhere that intense rush of pain came again, causing him to squeal in agony while the monstrous Melsean chuckled in his demonic overture.

"Oh, I forgot to mention that I had a few problems, well, more than a few you probably noticed. Anyway, in the process of nailing you, and I don't mean that in a gay sense because I'm a *straight* demon, some nails went through you due to your moving. However, I bet you're curious about my reasons for having these bottles and glue gun, aren't you?"

Sergeant McCray stared blankly at him as he watched Melsean plug the gun in.

"Of course, you are, so let me explain." He grabbed the first bottle. "It was said in Matthew 27:27 that the soldiers of the governor took Jesus into the governor's headquarters where they stripped him and put a scarlet robe on him." He reached out and grabbed one of the sleeves causing Sergeant McCray to wince in pain. "But like I said, I'm a straight demon, so what you're wearing is all right in my book. Anyway, after twisting some thorns into a crown, they put it on his head. You're wondering what you and Jesus could possibly have in common, aren't you? It's simple really—Jesus sacrificed his life for mankind, and you put your life on the line everyday. The governor considered Jesus the king of the Jews, you, on the other hand, are most certainly the sergeant of the fourth division riot squad. The point of this historic lesson is if Jesus can be killed in such a torturous and malicious manner and be who he was, then surely a man of your status would love nothing more than to be honored by the same method of death."

Melsean then pulled out a headband, picking up the glue gun in the same motion, and broke the bottle against the living room wall. He applied some of the hot glue along the inside of the band and then pressed it against the glass on the floor.

"Being there are no thorn bushes in here, I guess it's all right to use glass instead," Melsean cackled.

Sergeant McCray was having mixed emotions now. He didn't know which he should fear the most, Melsean's appearance or what he had in store for him. After the last touch of glue dried, sealing the small shards of glass in it, Melsean placed it with the glass-crusted side against McCray's head causing him to cry out in pain.

"Please, please don't! I have a..."

"You have nothing!" Melsean said, screwing up his face then softening it. "Besides, I haven't finished my story; trust me, it gets better." He reached out and grabbed another bottle and broke it almost to the neck of the bottle. He then rammed the shard through the right hand of Sergeant MCCray, causing him to bellow out in agony. Melsean reached for the third bottle, breaking it in the same motion, while using one hand to hold the shard in place and the other in a fist. He hammered the piece almost effortlessly as he'd done the first. By this time, Sergeant MCCray was slipping in and out of consciousness, but more in a catatonic state. He was losing a lot of blood and the pain was too much to bear.

"Jesus!" he cried out, thinking of the horrid sacrifice that Jesus endured for mankind. Considering the suffering of the Christ, he felt he could have done better about attending mass.

Melsean hammered the next broken bottle into his feet this time and was mesmerized by the blood collecting and spilling over the top of the bottle. His victim was fading quickly. Melsean reached up and grabbed him by his cheeks and squeezed.

"Stay with me, Sergeant. We're nearing the end of the story." He then paused briefly to recollect himself. "After Jesus yielded up his spirit from the cross—which isn't the case with you—and since it was preparation day, the Jews did not want the bodies left on the cross during the Sabbath, so they asked Pilate to have the legs of the crucified men broken and bodies removed. Then the soldiers came and broke the legs of the two men on the crosses beside Christ—it's a pity you're dying alone—but when they came to Jesus and saw that he was already dead..." Melsean picked up the remaining empty bottle and broke it.

Sergeant McCray never considered himself a religious man, but today he prayed, begging God for a quick death.

"...they did not break his legs. Instead, one of the soldiers pierced his side with a spear," he said ramming the broken bottle through Sergeant McCray's side, ripping through his lungs and immediately separating him from this world. Melsean looked at the Sergeant McCray's lifeless corpse thoughtfully, uttering, "You're no Jesus. After this death, there is no returning from the grave. See you in hell!" he said laughing uncontrollably while leaving the house and entering the cool night.

Eight

*I*sabella sat in the cool kitchen with her hands folded in front of her as she waited for the light and beep to inform her that the whole wheat bread she baked was done. She had prepared a beautiful dinner for her and Melsean which consisted of baked Rosemary chicken, seasoned baby red potatoes with a side of buttered artichoke hearts, and for dessert, a nice dish of banana pudding. The time was nearing seven o'clock. Isabella checked her watch. Melsean had been gone for hours and hadn't bothered to at least check in to let her know he was okay. *I'll give him fifteen more minutes before I jump to any conclusions and bring the authorities into it,* she thought. The time now was 7:07 p.m. and still there was no sign of Melsean. She began pacing her kitchen floor, checking her pots, pans, and other culinary equipment to avert her attention away from the fact of Melsean being missing-in-action. Again, looking at her watch, it was now

7:14 with ten seconds and going and she had become restless. Walking over to the phone, she proceeded to dial when a low, familiar humming from her car engine sounded followed by an indistinct one pulled into her driveway. She hurried to the window and was shocked to find Melsean idling her car before cutting the engine. Shaking her head, she peered at her watch and then did a double take because according to her watch it had just turned 7:15 on the nose. *Maybe it's a coincidence*, she thought, *one of tiffs smaller enigmas.* Laughing it off, she dismissed the thought just as fast as she had it.

She went outside to greet Melsean and whomever he had with him. Heading for the front entrance, she opened the door and walked out into the crimson-hued night.

"Hey there. I see you made it back. What happened?"

Melsean turned to face her and was immediately captivated. He didn't know what it was about her that demanded his attention, all he knew was that he had to yield to it.

"I'm sorry I took so long. My intentions were to pick up my friend," he pointed, "so that he could drive my car back here for me. Of course things didn't work as planned. First, I had to track my friend down. By the way, where are my manners?" he motioned for his friend to come over. Isabella prepared herself to speak to the man, but couldn't really see him because of the darkened distance between them. The only thing she could make out was that the person was wearing some kind of crew suit.

"Isabella Danpier, meet Andy Devilga."

Isabella stuck her hand out to shake the man's hand. "Hi. It's a pleasure to meet you, Andy, sir." She was met by the soft grip and warm face of a woman.

"Likewise, I'm sure, Isabella."

Isabella stepped back startled. "Oh my, I'm sorry, I didn't...I mean...I couldn't..."

"It's not your fault, Isabella," Andy said tapping the hand that was still in her grip. "You couldn't have known, especially with me wearing this crew suit and my hair tucked into it.

Despite the Carhartt crew suit and Timberland chukka boots Andy was wearing, Isabella was amazed at how beautiful the young lady was. She looked to be between the ages twenty-five and thirty, about 5'6" inches high, and one hundred and ten pounds. Her hair was an alluring brown tone with honey-blond streaks generously spread throughout the highlights of her hair. Her breasts were a thirty-two *D* easy; bulging against the fabric of her crew suit. If the rest of her body looked anywhere as good as her hands then the woman was flawless.

"So, how do you plan to get home, Andy?" Isabella asked with a light hint of concern.

"Oh, that's no problem. I have an employee who's going to be driving one of my company's trucks and should be here in a while."

"Well, at least come inside and have something to eat and drink until he gets here. I've got more than enough food."

"She doesn't have time," Melsean stated as a matter of fact. "Besides, the truck will be here shortly."

"Nonsense," Isabella chided. "Even if he will be here momentarily, how long do you think it would take to eat? Please, I insist."

"Well, I guess a few bites wouldn't hurt."

"No!" Melsean shouted. "It isn't good to keep Freddy waiting."

"Who's Freddy?" Isabella asked.

"Oh, Frederick is the guy who's driving my truck over to get me," Andy said, looking back and forth between Isabella and Melsean, then turned around to face the sound of an idling truck engine.

"Well, looks like my ride's here. I believe I'm going to have to take a rain check on our dinner plans."

"Yes, I suppose you're right," Isabella said, puzzled by Melsean's behavior. "I'll be looking forward to seeing you again."

"Count on it," Andy said, walking over toward the truck with Melsean trailing behind her.

Isabella watched them from the other end of her driveway as Melsean whispered something to Andy. She wondered just how close the two of them really were. *This is madness,* she thought. *How am I going to get jealous over a man I barely know and who doesn't belong to me? And what's worse is that he's my client?* She looked away concealing her embarrassment.

After a moment, Andy jumped into the truck, said her good-byes to Melsean, and waved at

Isabella. The truck then slowly began backing out of the driveway and took off into the night, beeping its horn as a final farewell to the two standing in the driveway. As soon as the truck's taillights vanished, Melsean turned to face Isabella, then proceeded to walk toward her. Kicking at invisible rocks and contemplating what he might say next, Isabella decided to make the first move.

"Well, she seems interesting."

"Oh, why do you say that?"

"Because it's not everyday that you find a woman who works for an auto shop. It's very liberating."

"Actually, she doesn't work for anybody. She owns it."

"Really? I'm impressed. That's one more facet conquered by women in this testosterone-driven society to brag about," she said, folding her arms around her breast and rubbing them.

"You're cold. Let's go inside and finish our discussion where it's warm."

She nodded in agreement, as Melsean wrapped his arm around her back and lightly massaged her arm as they made their way into the house. Melsean took in the pleasant aroma of vanilla bliss air freshener that mingled into one pleasant aroma. His stomach concurred with his olfactory assessment as it growled loud enough for Isabella to hear.

"I take it you're hungry?"

"Famished," he said, clutching his stomach as if he could truly hold the growling at bay with his mere hands.

"Listen, dinner is ready, so why don't you go and wash up a bit and I'll set the plates. The washcloths and towels are in the closet next to the bathroom, which is up the steps, down the hallway, second door on the right. Got it?"

"Got it."

"Good. I'll see you in a few," Isabella said, turning away from him and walking toward the kitchen.

Melsean went up the steps as directed by Isabella, moving down the hallway slowly in an attempt to take in all of the scenery. He marveled at the pictures and portraits on the wall. Some revealed pictures of Isabella as young as about eighteen. *She's breathtaking*, Melsean thought, eying one of her more professional photos from a real photographer, but what really caught his attention was a photo of her with a man who appeared to be around six years older than her. They were sharing a giant alpine white chocolate bar at Hershey Park, which was obvious given everybody were either eating chocolate or wearing Hershey's shirts and caps. *This man appeared to be happy, but who wouldn't if they had a woman like Isabella? She's smart, sexy, and stable—it doesn't get much better than that.*

"Hey, what happened? Did you get lost?" she asked from the bottom of the stairs.

Melsean broke away from his thoughts and peered down at his watch and was shocked to find that he'd been staring at that same photo for almost ten minutes.

"Are you all right?" she asked again.

This time he responded. "Yes. Of course, I'm fine. I'll be down in a minute, okay?"

"Okay, but hurry. I know you don't want to eat cold food, do you?"

"No, but I'm sure if you make it hot or cold it's still going to be delicious."

"You're a liar—a good liar—but a liar nonetheless, and I'm flattered. Don't be long." She turned and headed back to the kitchen.

Melsean decided not to waste anymore time, so he went on and got himself a washcloth and matching hand towel, turned on the steaming hot water, and began to wash off. He had his face almost in the sink as he generously lathered it with soap and rinsed it off. He repeated this method two more times to be sure that he had gotten the stench of Central booking out of the pores of his face; there was nothing he could do about the rest of his body at the moment, but he would take care of that immediately after dinner and as soon as he retrieved his bags from the car. He turned off the water and blindly reached for the hand towel and patted his face dry. He then raised his head, at the same time opening his eyes, and dropped the hand towel in the sink out of shock of what fell upon his eyes. He knew Isabella was not safe as long as he was there due to the words written on the steamed mirror which read... *They All Must Pay!*

Nine

*D*etective Donovan Lynch rubbed his eyes as he took long gulps of strong, black coffee. He hated to be disturbed when he was sleeping. For two months, he had been working on a double homicide that took place in Oceanville Terrace, in Brooklyn, over a drug sting headed by him that went sour; leaving two undercover officers dead. The New York Police Commissioner had personally chewed him a new asshole after Internal Affairs had their way with him, and he was given two months to close the case or be indefinitely demoted back to rookie status or permanently kicked off the force without pay or benefits.

Donavan had already made arrangements to secure positions in other fields of work when, on the last day of his deadline, he was rewarded with the voluntary confession from the killer of both officers. This not only secured his employment, but made headlines in every newspaper in the tri-state region.

Donavan was enjoying his moment in the spotlight tonight when he had received a call from one of his fellow detectives that a neighbor of the deceased had heard a nerve-biting shriek that sounded like nothing she had heard before, and decided to call the authorities. He came to the front entrance of the deceased's home. Ducking under the yellow tape, while balancing his coffee as not to spill it, he flagged down the nearest officer to him.

"Who's in charge here?"

"Who wants to know?" the officer asked back, eying him from head to toe.

"Detective Donavan Lynch, Homicide Division, you fucking prick," he said, whipping out his badge. "What's your name, son?"

"Officer Sheldon Smith, sir," he said in a shaky voice, exposing his anxiety.

"Okay, Officer Smith, I can see that you're a little wet behind the ears, so I'm going to ask you for the last time, who-the fuck-is in charge?"

"Sorry, sir," the officer said, stuttering between every word. "Officer Davis was the first on the scene and was given authorization to head this case and secure all potential evidence."

"Is that right?" Donavan asked sarcastically. "Well, there's been new orders since then. As of now, I am in charge," he flashed a sheet of paper at the officer, "so from now on, you take orders from no one but me, unless I say otherwise. Do we have a clear understanding?"

"Yes, sir!"

"Good. Now go hurry and bring Officer Davis to me, so I can relieve him of his duties."

"Yes, sir," Officer Smith said, walking away from Detective Lynch.

"Oh, and Sheldon," Donavan said, causing Sheldon to turn abruptly and face him.

"Yes?"

"You're not moving fast enough. I said hurry!"

Officer Smith then took off running in search of Davis.

"And bring me a fresh cup of black," he yelled behind the man. Donavan then turned to another officer and began to question him.

"So, what's the situation here?"

"Jesus Christ," the officer responded.

"I beg your pardon?"

"The victim—that's who he was treated like," he said, pointing to the chalked outline of the body that was traced where it had been on the wall. There were four holes in the wall with shards of glass protruding from them; one in the center of the palm prints on both hands, one where both feet were joined and nailed together, and a light impression on the right side of the drawing just below where its ribs were.

"Gee wiz. Who the hell could've done that, and what are those tiny holes inside the tracing?"

"Well, the holes you're referring to were made from nails that were also holding the body up against the wall. As for who could've done it, beats the hell out of me."

"Detective Donavan moved closer to the wall

and examined the distance between where the deceased's feet were nailed down to the floor. It was approximately four feet.

"Holy mother of blessings. How did they get him all the way up there?"

"They? What makes you think it was more than one?"

"Because no one man can lift a man, four feet at that, and nail him to a wall at the same time."

"Nothing human at least," Officer Davis cut in, making his way toward Donavan with Sheldon Smith trailing behind him, carrying a mug of steaming coffee as the detective requested. "I don't believe we've met. I'm Officer Davis..." he said, extending his hand, "and you are?"

"Detective Donavan Lynch, Homicide Division," he said while grabbing hold of the man's hand in a firm grip and shook it. "I'm sure your colleague Officer Smith here informed you of my taking over this case, right?"

"Yes, he did mention something to that effect, but as you can see, I have the situation under control, and don't need your assistance."

"I'm sure you don't," he said as he put his arm around the officer and passed him a sheet with precise orders on it. "Listen, Officer Davis, I didn't come down here to bust your balls or question your competence. I was sent to take over this investigation, but being the nice man that I am, I am offering you the opportunity to assist me in this investigation and earn yourself a promotion to a detective. How does that sound to you?"

Officer Davis threw his hands on his waist as if really contemplating what was just said forcing Donavan to break the silence.

"So?" he asked impatiently.

"So, do I really have a choice?"

"Of course, you do. Only one is not such a good one."

"Fine," Officer Davis said defeated. "We'll play this your way. You're in charge. What's our first move?"

"Well, first thing, thank you," he said taking the mug of coffee from Officer Smith. "I need to know the occupation of the deceased and find out if he had any enemies."

"You don't know, do you?" Officer Davis asked.

"Know what? We don't have time for the guessing game. What do you know that I don't?"

"For starters, the deceased is Sergeant Matthew McCray from the New York Riot Squad Division, so it could have been anybody with a mug shot."

"Dammit! Okay, get in touch with One Police Plaza and tell them I want the names and photo arrays of every released felon that was known to be in good physical shape. Next, I want the same on every felon or felon busted by Sergeant MCCray that dealt in occultism." Donavan's eyes examined the entire living room looking for hints or signs of a struggle, but saw nothing out of the norm.

"Any evidence turn up?"

"Not yet, but forensics are fine combing the

crime scene looking for prints and other unseen evidence. Give them some time, I'm sure they'll find something."

"I hope so because for some strange reason, I have a feeling that I'm not going to like how this turns out." He turned to Officer Smith. "Hey, Sheldon, you told me earlier that a neighbor said she heard some kind of sound?"

"A shriek, sir."

"Same thing."

"Apparently not to her. She insisted that we call it just that—a shriek."

Donavan rubbed his stubble face as he pondered on what was just said. "Well, I guess it's time to pay our special witness a visit, don't you think? What's her name and where exactly is she?"

"Her name is Nancy Stevens. She's about fifty-eight-years-old, retiree, and she lives with her pet cat. Her house is next door to the right. Got it?"

"Yes, but I want you to come with me just in case and, Davis, you stay here and see to it forensics finds something. We can't have murderous thugs running around gunning down our own, can we?"

"Oh, and Detective, we have one more problem."

"Yeah, and what might that be?"

"Well, remember when you sent me to get Officer Davis and your cup of coffee?"

"Yes, go on."

"Okay, well, on my way back, I noticed the Channel 21 news van outside and I believe they've spoken to Ms. Stevens. However," he said raising his hand to keep Donavan from cutting him off, "they haven't aired anything as of yet."

"Then I guess it's best that we get over there and hold them off for a while and get the scoop from Ms. Stevens before this investigation goes sour."

They headed outside but it was too late. The news reporter was broadcasting the murder as a special report. This was not going to help the case. Donavan turned to Sheldon Smith and gave him a cold stare that silently spoke his frustrations, causing Sheldon to cringe in defense.

"I didn't know."

Donavan just shook his head disbelievingly as he made his way to Nancy's home in hopes of salvaging some type of leverage in this investigation. He desperately hoped that Sergeant McCray's murder wasn't turned into the eight o'clock news.

Ten

Isabella smiled to herself as she washed the dishes. She and Melsean had shared a beautiful dinner. He enjoyed the chicken and had practically worshipped her banana pudding. He wasn't too fond of the artichokes, but that was to be expected. Melsean was the best houseguest she'd ever had over. She appreciated the way he helped her clean off the table and put away the food. Now he was helping her wash and dry the dishes.

She wondered if this was what it would be like to be married to him. He was handsome, charismatic, physically alluring, and had good home ethics and mannerisms. But of course, the reality is that he was her client and lawyers weren't supposed to court them. *Nonsense*, she thought. *Why else would the Judge make her bring her client home if he didn't see some type of chemistry between the two of them.* She stared at Melsean as he dried the last plate, allowing her eyes to wander from his face down to his torso and lingering in the crotch area.

Melsean caught her watching him. He didn't mind, nor did he feel the slightest twinge of discomfort. Truth be told, he was watching her as well. He loved her light complexion; it complimented her sandy-brown hair and hourglass figure. She looked like one of those women straight out of a beauty pageant and she knew how to work that thing without working it; Melsean could tell.

"What are you looking at?" Melsean asked, causing Isabella to be jolted upright.

"Nothing. I was..."

"Looking at my Johnson, I know," he said hiding his amusement.

"I was not...okay, I was, but not the way you think I was."

"Oh really? I assume this is where you concoct some fancy legal scenario that'll explain why you were recklessly eyeballing my crotch."

"No, see—you know what," she sighed. "I was going to explain, but I see you already have all the answers, so I'll keep them to myself and let you draw your own conclusions." Isabella dried off her hands, turned off the running water, and looked at her watch. It was 7:58 p.m.

"Come on Melsean. The news is about to begin and I don't like to miss the headlines." She walked out of the kitchen and Melsean followed behind her. They sat down on her beige, leather love seat. Isabella reached for the remote on the coffee table and pressed one of her memory buttons that automatically changed the channel to 21 just in time to catch the beginning. News anchorwoman Penelope Fleming appeared on the screen and began her broadcasting.

"Good evening everyone. I am Penelope Fleming, bringing you today's latest events. Now for the breaking news. Police officials are investigating the gruesome murder of Sergeant Matthew McCray, the team leader for the New York City Riot Squad Division. Reporter Jasmine Diaco has the coverage."

A fair skinned Italian woman appeared on the screen. She looked to be anywhere between twenty-seven and thirty-two years of age with a very mild voice.

"Thank you, Penelope, and what a gruesome scene it is. Never in my career of reporting have I heard of such a heinous act. An eyewitness to the crime says she heard a loud shriek coming from Sergeant McCray's home and decided to call the authorities. She went over to the deceased's house to see if he needed assistance. What she found was McCray's lifeless body nailed to the wall where he was literally crucified like Christ. Sources say Sergeant McCray was responsible for the shooting and arrest of Shuster and Johnson's financial analyst Melsean Natas, who was recently charged with the murder of his girlfriend Annette Simmons. He was released today on his own recognizance. Detective Duncan Reese was called in to head the investigation. So far, there have been no leads, but Detective Reese is asking if anyone has information on the death of Sergeant McCray, to please contact him or call 1-800-tips. More information will be given as it

comes in. I'm Jasmine Diaco for Channel 21 news at eight."

Isabella stared blankly at the TV, unsure of her next move. She wanted to look at Melsean, but her eyes would not permit her. Too many thoughts were running through her mind, bombarding one on top of the next, rendering her confused and asphyxiated with questions.

Melsean, too, stared at the TV blankly, but there was no mistaking what he was feeling at that moment. Tears welled in his eyes as he fought to control his emotions. *What must Isabella be thinking of me now?* he wondered. It hasn't even been ten hours since his release and already they are implicating him for yet another homicide. This has got to stop. He feared the idea of looking at or even talking to Isabella, but he knew it wasn't in his best interest to give her enough time to let her imagination run wild. He turned to her.

"I assume you're feeling a little mixed up with tonight's events, aren't you?"

"Yeah, you can say that," she said rubbing her throbbing temples, still staring at the TV screen but not watching it.

"I know I should tell you something, but I have so many thoughts running through my head right now. I don't even know where to begin."

"Well you can begin by explaining where you were this afternoon when you took off, and next you can explain how your dead girlfriend wound up as a human barbecue."

"I told you I didn't do it," Melsean said clenching his hands into fists so tight that he almost drew blood.

"Listen, I never said you did anything, but you cannot negate the fact that you were in fact at your girlfriend's house and standing over her flaming body. Now please, tell me where you went this afternoon."

"Like I said before, I had an appointment with a friend."

"Let me guess, Andy, right?"

"Right."

"Okay, go on."

"As you know, I lost my apartment due to me getting shot and being held in a prison hospital ward. I went first to see the super of my building and he told me he put my property in storage and that I would have to pay to get it out."

"And that's where Andy came in the picture, isn't it?"

"Well yeah. I mean after all, she did have my car. It was being ticketed, but I wasn't there to move it, so Andy picked it up and stored it in her garage at her auto shop. That's what I went out to do this afternoon, but I figured since I had no clothes over here, I'd get Andy to foot the bill for my storage. I only took out a couple of weeks worth of clothes until I could find a place of my own."

Those words stung Isabella as she sat with her left leg folded under her. She knew that sooner or later he was going to pack up and leave, but it wasn't until now that the reality of those words hit her. *Nonsense*, she thought. *You hardly know the guy.*

How could you possibly feel something for a stranger? "Okay, so where are these clothes?"

"Oh, that's right!" he said, snapping his fingers. "I left them in the car. I was so anxious to get back that I forgot to pull them out."

"Well, it's getting late, so maybe we should go and bring your stuff in. Besides, I know you'd like to wash that jail junk out of your pores, right?"

"You know what, you've absolutely read my mind," he said, lifting from the couch with a smile.

"No, actually I picked up your scent. You smell like a cross between a wet ashtray and a copout sandwich," she said as she raised her hands, fanned at Melsean, and walked ahead of him. "I hope that you're aware that April is not going to like that you didn't even try her cobbler."

"Who's April, and what cobbler are you talking about?" Melsean asked puzzled.

"Don't worry," she said. "You'll meet her tomorrow. Let's just concentrate on the funk right now, Bootsy."

"Ha, very funny, Bella. But you don't smell so Au Bon Pain yourself," and they both laughed on their way to the car.

Eleven

onavan left Nancy Steven's house fuming. He was partly mad that Jasmine Diaco from Channel 21 had released information on the case, upset that some numbskull fuck head had leaked information to that nosey bitch about Ms. Stevens, and most importantly, pissed off at Sheldon Smith for not informing him earlier about the happenings. This whole investigation was going to hell, but the worst part of it was that it was still fresh. Normally, if a trail goes cold in the beginning, it usually doesn't make a change for the better.

So far, the only clue he had to go on was a brief description given by Ms. Stevens that fits Melsean's description to a tee. He turned to Officer Smith.

"All right, Sheldon, I'm going to need you to come with me to Ms. Danpier's house."

"You mean Isabella Danpier, the famous defense attorney? That Isabella Danpier? Why?"

"Well, word has it that Melsean Natas was released into the custody of Ms. Danpier, therefore, wherever Ms. Danpier is, that's where we'll find Melsean."

"I'll tell you one thing..." Officer Davis interjected, "if she is who you and Sheldon say she is, I doubt she's going to be happy with you winding up at her house as this time of night."

"What? Are you suggesting that we wait until morning and give Mr. I-can-kill-when-I-feel-like-it, enough time to get rid of important evidence?"

"First of all, we have no warrant, so anything you find or expect to find will hold no weight in court. My advice is that we wait until morning and if you feel like questioning him, fine, but at least we won't have to suffer the wrath of a pissed off attorney. So, what do you say? It's your call."

Normally Donavan would have stuck out his chest and exercised his power as lead of an investigation, but fact is fact—fucking with Melsean tonight would definitely cause shit to roll down hill, and in this case, he was the one standing at the bottom.

"Fine, we'll wait. But if someone else drops dead before this investigation comes to a head, I'm going to nail his ass to the wall just like Sergeant McCray...no offense."

"None taken," Davis said, hiding his smirk behind his hand.

"I want Melsean in this office for questioning by ten o'clock tomorrow morning, which means I expect to see two ticked off faces when I walk into that interrogation room. Are we clear on that?"

Both men nodded in agreement.

"Good, then let's wrap this up and call it a night, fellows. The coroner took the body to the morgue to be autopsied, the crime scene has been secured, and potential evidence is being collected as we speak. We should have something solid by tomorrow."

"Detective Lynch, we've found something!" one of his officers said, running with something dangling in a plastic evidence bag.

"Or we may even have something solid tonight. What did you find in there?"

"See for yourself," the man said, passing the bag over to Donavan. There was a solid gold initial plate, bearing two alphabets entwined together. They were all too familiar to Detective Lynch.

MN

Donavan held the bag in front of Davis' face, making sure that he'd seen every detail of the evidence before him.

"So, you mean to tell me that even with this..." he pointed at the bag, "we don't have probably cause to haul his ass in for questioning?"

"No, Detective," Davis said, pushing the plastic bag out of his face. "What I said was that even if you found something, without a warrant, it wouldn't hold any weight in court because it was unlawfully attained. This, on the other hand, makes a world of a difference, but I want no part of it because something isn't right here...it just don't make sense."

"Good. Then you can stay here and hold down the fort until it does. Sheldon, I guess it's me and you. My car or yours?"

"Let's take mine. It has a six cylinder engine."

"Sounds like a plan to me. Let's go. Oh, Davis, be sure that I have your report on tonight's homicide on my desk before I get in tomorrow, understood?"

"Yes, sir," Officer Davis said waiting for Detective Lynch to turn around before he gave him the middle finger, causing Sheldon to snicker to himself.

"Give me your keys, I'm driving," Donavan said, as they neared Sheldon's car. Sheldon passed him the keys and they got in and pulled away from the curb. Donavan reached into his pocket and pulled out a bottle of Rolaids. Sheldon stared at Donavan as he popped the bottle, took out two pills, and chewed the dry, chalky pills with no liquid, and closed the bottle in the same motion. From the looks of it, one could safely assume that Detective Lynch was no stranger to stress, ulcers, and acid reflux. However, given what happened today, one would seriously suspect that he was far from finished indulging.

Twelve

Isabella and Melsean sat in silence, watching UPN's eight o'clock movie *Lost Soul* as it drew to an end. Isabella wasn't what you would call a diehard horror fan. She sat with her legs curled underneath her and her arms folded as if she had a chill in her bones.

Melsean side-glanced at her and noticed her discomfort and decided to embrace her. At first she resisted his attempt to draw her near, but she soon eased the tension and allowed herself to fall into the warmth of his body.

"This is weird," Isabella said. "I never thought I'd ever be in the arms of one of my clients."

"You're not alone there. Of course, I can't say that I never fantasized about being with one of my lawyers."

"One of your lawyers?"

"Well yeah, it's not like you were my first counselor," he said grinning.

"Oh, is that all you see me as?" she said, lightly punching him until she fell deeply into his grasp. She looked into his eyes and couldn't help the urge of wanting to make love to him. She tried everything in her power to resist it, but she couldn't break the spell he had cast over her. The mouth between her legs was smacking its lips and drooling for a taste of his masculinity.

Melsean was feeling the same way about her. The woman was giving off pheromones left and right. *It's strange how one day can stir hidden emotions between two people—strangers at that*, he thought. He was enthralled by the way her breast heaved against her silk blouse, exposing a pair of unusually large nipples. They moved their faces closer, leaving only a thin layer of space between them, staking in the warmth of each other's breath until finally their lips met in one wet motion. He removed his hands from the nape of her neck and gently slid them from her shoulders to her breasts and cupping them from underneath. He proceeded to gently massage them.

Isabella's pulse quickened as she allowed her body to submit to the will of Melsean. Her inner voice was warning her that if she didn't stop now, there'd be no stopping, but she didn't care. Melsean's free hand made its way down to the zipper of her pants, slowly unzipping it to gain entry to her nether region, but found himself restricted by the tight and close fit of Isabella's pants. Out of frustration, Melsean unfastened the button, stuck his hand into her panties, and cupped her wet, hairy mound. His index and middle finger slid deep into the satiny slit, causing Isabella to slump on the couch and spread wider to give him more control of his motion.

"We shouldn't be doing this," Melsean whispered into her ear.

"Why? Who's here to stop us?" she whispered back.

"This goes against all professional ethics."

"Then let the judge hold me in contempt of court, but it's his fault that you're here in the first place." She unzipped Melsean's pants and reached into his boxers and released his engorged member. She spat in her hand and gently massaged Melsean's rod, meticulously stroking it as to not bring him to a premature climax, only to tease him. Melsean, sensing what she was doing, plunged his fingers deeper inside her, then curled them, causing Isabella to moan in pleasure and stroke him more vigorously. Both were nearing to completion when all of a sudden the phone rang. Isabella rose with a start and lost her orgasm. Melsean, too, was thrown off by the tumult of the phone as Isabella rushed off to answer it.

"Hello?" she said in an agitated tone.

"Hey, Isabella. It's me."

"Oh, Kayman," she raved. "Why is it that you always disturb me when I'm busy?"

"I'm sorry. So what were you doing?"

"It's personal."

"I see. Do you mean personal like bringing your client home with you to stay? Is that the kind of personal you're talking about?"

"That was the judge's idea, not mine, and what exactly are you implying?"

"Not a thing. I was just messing with you. I got the word from your secretary. What's her name?"

"Rhonda!" Isabella snapped. "Since when did you build a good enough rapport with my secretary to pump information from her?"

"Jeez, Issey, you're getting yourself all riled up for nothing. Am I not supposed to be concerned about you? If not, I apologize, but I was truly under the impression that we were friends."

Isabella lightened her grip on the telephone as she absorbed what Kayman had just said to her. *Way to go Isabella,* she thought. *I feel like a piece of shit right now.* "Look, I'm sorry, Kayman. I have just been under a lot of pressure lately and it is now at its peak, but that's no reason for me to lash out at you. Can you forgive me?"

"I don't know," Kayman said in a pouting tone. "You really hurt my feelings. I mean, of course, there is one thing you could do to make it up to me."

"Really," she said, not trusting his tone. "And what might that be?"

"Don't worry. I'll come up with something."

"Oh," she said realizing Melsean was still in the room. "My client Melsean is right here. Would you like to introduce yourself?"

Melsean began reaching for the phone when the weirdest feeling came over him, causing his hand to stop in its track.

"Nah, save it for another day. Besides, I

haven't explained to you my reason for calling yet."

Isabella looked at the phone puzzled, then insatiably placed it back to her ear as Melsean looked on with a note of curiosity.

"I know that tone, Kayman. What happened?"

"You mean you missed the news again?"

"No, I caught it this time. I was watching the eight o'clock headlines on channel twenty-one about sergeant McCray's murder."

"Brutal, huh?"

"That's an understatement to what they say happened to him—I mean, my God, some psycho-sadistic son-of-a-bitch crucified the man. Do you know how crazy that sounds? Who would do something crazy like that?"

"That's what I wanted to talk to you about. It seems the police have a feeling that your client knows something about the murder."

"Wait a minute, slow down. What are you saying here?"

"I'm saying that the authorities believe that Melsean either did the murder or is closely involved."

Isabella turned and looked at Melsean with a note of worry on her face. "That's bull. They have nothing to substantiate that claim."

Melsean noticed the look on Isabella's face and immediately knew that she and her friend were talking about him and it wasn't good.

"What is it, Isabella? What is he saying?"

Isabella threw her hand up in a gesture to tell Melsean to hold fast.

"Quite the contrary, Issey. Word has it that a

chain of some sort was found clenched in the hand of sergeant McCray and a gold name plate was found at the scene bearing the initials M and N connected together."

"That doesn't mean he did it."

"True, but it does give probable cause, not to mention we're talking about the death of the man that shot and arrested your client. I'd say they have every right to suspect him."

"Listen, I don't want to hear anymore of this."

"If you want me to shut up about it, fine. I'll do that, but I'll bet you're going to hear more about this within the hour."

"What are you saying?"

"I'm saying Detective Reese and a few of his friends are on their way to question your client. Whether they intend to arrest him or not is beyond me, but believe me when I say they're coming."

Melsean was becoming more worried by the second. Every time he inquired about Isabella's conversation with her friend, he was either ignored or she signaled to him to wait and he was tired of that. He was fully aware that their conversation was solely based on him; that much he gathered from her expressions and her hushed, discreet manner. This time, enough was enough.

"Listen, Isabella, what's going on? I know you two are talking about me, so let's skip the put-off session and tell me what the matter is. I have a right to know if it's about me."

Isabella removed the phone from her ear and muffled the mouthpiece of the phone. "Melsean, give me a second to get rid of Kayman and I promise that I will answer all of your questions, okay?"

He nodded his head in approval. She then placed the phone back to her ear and ended the call with Kayman. "Listen, I have to get prepared for my guest and bring my client up to speed with what's happening. I'll call you tomorrow morning, okay?"

"I'll be waiting for your call. Goodnight and be careful," he said cutting the connection off between them. Isabella hung up as well.

"So?" Melsean prodded.

Isabella sat on the bed with her back facing Melsean as she stared at his reflection in her dresser's mirror and began grooming her hair. "So, it appears we're about to have a few guests over."

"Yeah, who?"

"A Detective Lynch, I was told. With whom, I have no idea. All I know is that they're on their way to talk to you."

"About?" Melsean asked with a slight touch of sarcasm.

"Well, to begin with, they want to know where you were at the time of Sergeant McCray's murder and why they found a gold plate bearing your initials on it."

"My initials," he mumbled, puzzled by this revelation of events. "I don't have a chain with an initial plate."

"I know, Melsean, and I believe you. But it's not me you have to convince, it's Detective Lynch," she said, twisting a scrungee around her hair and binding it into a ponytail. "Listen, they're going to be here soon, so you might as well go and clean yourself up before they come."

Melsean turned and was about to walk out of the room, but stopped in mid stride with his arms outstretched against the threshold of the room.

"Look, Isabella, about what happened a little while ago."

"I'm not sorry it happened, are you?"

"No, I just needed to know that you feel the same way about me as I feel about you."

"Melsean, I would love to discuss us, but now is hardly the time. We need to focus on what you're going to tell Detective Lynch when he gets here, because if he's anything like me, he'll smell a lie like a week-old corpse and pick it clean like a vulture."

"Okay, okay, I get your point. I'll be in the bathroom cleaning up."

Isabella just stared into the mirror. She wanted to believe Melsean, but so far everything was pointing to him as the killer. *It couldn't just be a coincidence that the killer just so happened to bear the same initials as Melsean—or could it?*

Thirteen

*D*esiree Wilson rolled over to the right side of the bed, sat up, and wiped the thin film of sweat from her brow. She then reached for her Newports on her nightstand, patted one out, placed it in her mouth, and lit it. She took a long pull, and then looked down to her left at the young man beside her. Desiree marveled at his muscular frame as he lay there in a deep slumber. *Poor baby*, she thought. She left the courtroom earlier, fuming over the release of Melsean Natas, and for some odd reason, felt it necessary to take this case, out of all her previous cases, personal.

The judge had no right to allow him to be released. People like Melsean should not be allowed a second chance to walk the streets and prey on some other innocent victim.

Desiree was so upset about Melsean's release that she decided to make a pit stop at Patty O'Malley's

Pub, located on the lower East side, where she indulged in multiple double shots of Seagram's Extra Dry Gin. After three hours of continuous drinking, the bartender closed the bar to her, causing Desiree to become erratic and curse at the bartender. He was about to kick her out when the young man beside her vouched that he would take responsibility for her and paid her tab. They did more drinking than talking between the two of them. Now that she thought about it, she couldn't recall ever getting the name of the man in her bed, or even mentioning hers. What she did remember was that she was totally ripped—a sniff hound would've become inebriated by the scent of her breath; she had eighty proof seeping out of her pores and the whole bedroom reeked of it.

She placed a hand between her legs and rubbed her sore and throbbing vagina. She felt something wet and brought it close to her face for inspection and found to her distaste a sickening combination of cum and clotted blood. Apparently the young stud wanted to prove he was a beast in bed, but truth was she didn't remember any of it. *I must've blacked out,* she thought, and it probably was a good thing because judging by the way she felt and what she observed. The young punk more than likely bent her cervix and now she'd pay during every menstrual cycle from then on.

She welcomed the quietness of her house next to the light snoring coming from the young jackhammer sleeping beside her as she puffed away at her cigarette. She stood up and walked over to the

window and stared at the pine trees that surrounded her Westchester home. From a distance, she
could hear the neighborhood strays communicating
amongst each other in some kind of sacred chant.
Other than that, there was a void of silence.
Suddenly, the portable phone beside her bed rang,
causing Desiree's bedroom guest to stir in his sleep.
She immediately grabbed the phone and stepped
out of the bedroom, closing the door behind her. She
walked down to the end of the hall, stopped at the
bend of her steps, and sat down.

"Hello?" she said in a dry, raspy voice.

"Am I speaking to District Attorney Desiree
Wilson?"

"Yes, this is she. And who am I speaking to?"

"This is Dr. Troy Benning from the New York
City Specimens Laboratory. I believe you were waiting for the results pertaining to a recent murder that
took place."

"Yes!" she said, snapping out of her drunken
stupor, but trying to keep the excitement out of her
voice as to not wake her guest. "Go on with your
findings, please."

He cleared his throat. "We've ran a series of
tests: Protein, fiber, follicle, you name it, we've done
it. However, we kept coming up with an inconclusive
reading."

"Inconclusive? Are you telling me that with all
that hi-tech equipment you people have, you can't
pinpoint this psycho's DNA in any of the collected
evidence?" She was becoming annoyed with their
conversation.

"No, I'm saying that what we're dealing with here is something extraordinary in itself. I've read about such things, but never thought them possible to actually exist."

"I'm not following. Where are you going with this?"

"Back in a time around 325 C.E., otherwise known as *Common Era*, Emporer Constantine called the first ecumenical counsel to deal with the issue of Homousios and Homoisios."

"Homo-eroowee, what? Is this a history lesson on homosexuality? What relevance does any of what you said have to do with this case?"

"Listen, Ms. Wilson, you asked me to give you a full report on my findings, right? Well, I suggest you close your mouth and listen intently because what I'm about to say is going to blow your mind."

Desiree wanted to say something snide, but thought against it. Her target was Melsean and she intended on burying him beneath the jail if she had anything to say about it. "Very well then. Please continue."

"Okay, basically the ecumenical council was called in the city of Nicea to deal with the issue of Christ's divinity—that's were Homousios and Homoisios come into place. The argument between the papacy, known today as popes, and priests were the issue as to whether Christ was of the same divine substance of God (Homousios) or of similar substance (Homoisios). Now my point to you, Ms. Wilson, is that after performing all the tests under the strict supervision of my superiors, they too have witnessed the same findings that I have."

Desiree became perplexed. "What you're saying is much too vague for my limited comprehension, Doctor. You're going to have to simplify, but be blunt at the same time if you expect me to be on the same page as you."

Dr. Benning sighed out loud in exasperation then searched his mental Webster for adequate diction to accommodate her. "What I'm saying, Ms. Wilson, is that what's going on here is a classic reenactment of that historical event; in laymen's term; you have a classic case of Homoisios going on."

"Doc?"

"You're dealing with someone of similar bimolecular structure as your perp."

"So, what are we dealing with, like some kind of twin?"

"Well, it's either that, or science is going to have to revamp and revise millions of books on DNA and fingerprinting because no one print is alike. In this case, it's identical all the way down to the inner-rings."

"If they're so similar, how is it that you can tell them apart?"

"Trust me, it wasn't simple. After doing a number of tests on the DNA and coming up with inconclusive results, I decided to test the subject's hormonal level and found that Melscan is secreting nothing but testosterone into his system. First off, those are not the samples you sent from the scene of the crime. These were collected and submitted by the Department of Corrections—yours, on the contrary, gave off both testosterone and estrogen, not to mention traces of highly concentrated lighter fluid. This means whoever murdered the deceased was not only a man, but a woman as well."

Desiree remained quiet on the line for a minute, in shock from what she had just heard, but asked again to be sure she didn't misunderstand him. "So he didn't commit the murder?"

"Uh uh."

"And I was..."

"Uh huh."

"So I should..."

"I would."

"Okay, thank you, Dr. Benning. You've been a tremendous help to me and I'll take care of this problem first thing in the morning."

"You're welcome, Ms. Wilson. I'll be sending you the analysis report FedEx by same-day service."

"Excellent, I'll be expecting it. Oh, and Dr. Benning?"

"Yes."

"Could you please send me a personal copy via my fax here at home?"

"Sure, no problem. What's your number?"

Desiree gave him the number and waited for the fax. Her head was troubled and she knew it wasn't because of the alcohol she had consumed earlier. If anything, it was because of the anxiety she was feeling knowing she had to now do the right thing and let Melsean go. Worse than that, she had to admit herself as being wrong and Isabella as right. *I should call her tonight*, she thought, *but what would*

I possibly tell her, that Melsean was innocent, but his mystery twin isn't?"

What she had to do was wait for the reports and take proof to Isabella of her findings and work from there. It was times like this where she really needed a scraping to take her mind off of the bull-shit. She stood up with the phone in hand and walked back down the hall to her bedroom to wake her young stud up for another helping of Peter-ala mode. Tomorrow's news could wait, but her hormones couldn't.

Fourteen

*D*etective Lynch pulled into the driveway of Isabella's home accompanied by Officer Sheldon Smith at 10:05 p.m. He looked through the cracks of the blinds in the windows and could see that somebody was still up. He shut off the ignition and turned to Officer Smith.

"Do I need to give you the 'I'm in charge and ask all the questions' speech?"

"No, sir. The ball is in your court. Bounce it where you may."

"Good. Then let's get this show on the road, shall we?"

Not waiting for an answer, Donavan got out of the car and advanced to the front door. Sheldon sat in the car a moment longer, then proceeded to the door behind Donavan. Detective Donavan rang the doorbell, then reached into his jeans and pulled out his badge. No sooner had he rung the bell, the sound of footsteps came followed by the opening of the door revealing

Isabella's face.

"Yes, may I help you?"

"Yes, I hope so. I'm looking for a Ms. Isabella Danpier. Is that you?"

"Who's inquiring?"

"Oh, forgive me. Where are my manners? I'm Detective Donavan Lynch, and this here is Officer Sheldon Smith," he pointed. "He's assisting me with this investigation."

"Okay, I should care about your so-called investigation because?"

"Not you necessarily, Ms. Danpier. We're more interested in your client." He pulled out his pad, checked for the name, then put it back in his pocket. "Melsean Natas."

"It's pronounced Nah-tay. He's French, but other than that, what does my client have to do with this investigation of yours?"

"Ms. Danpier, I would be more than happy to answer all of your questions, but not from the other side of your door. We'd simply like to speak to you and your client for a few minutes and then be on our way?"

"Do you have a warrant or legal sanction from the judge to question my client?"

"No, I don't, Ms. Danpier," Donavan said between clinched teeth, trying to hide his impatience. "I was hoping we could do this without judicial intervention."

Isabella enjoyed making the detective sweat. She intended to let them in eventually, but wasn't going to make it easy. Her first instincts were to play with his head a little, but seeing what was about to take place that didn't seem like a good idea. Besides, the last thing she wanted to do was piss off the investigating officer. Isabella widened the door and motioned the two officers in.

"I wasn't expecting any visitors tonight. I do have some peach cobbler that was just baked earlier today. I could fix both you gentlemen a helping with a fresh cup of coffee. How does that sound?"

"Sounds to me like you have too much free time on your hands."

"Is that a yes?"

"That's a definite yes," Donavan said.

"And what about you, Silent Smith? Care for a slice, or does a cat have your taste buds?"

Sheldon Smith stared nervously at Donavan as if waiting for his approval. Donavan, picking up the signal, shrugged his shoulders at the deputy officer in a carefree manner, so the young man nodded in acceptance.

"Good. I assume you both take sugar and cream in your coffee, right?"

They nodded in unison.

"Then it's settled. I'll go fix you gentlemen your cobblers and coffee and Melsean should be downstairs with us shortly. Please make yourselves at home," she motioned them to the couch in the living room. Officer Sheldon took a seat, while Detective Lynch decided to peruse the living room area. He admired her taste in style. Throughout the entire room there were collectable figurines from the likes of such companies as Franklin Mint and Lenox and Drake, all scattered and creating an ambiance of artistic bend. Above the mantle of the fireplace was a portrait of Edvard Munch's *The Scream*, which Detective Lynch took as a symbol of what most defense lawyers feel like doing in court when confronted by the harsh realities of the so-called justice system. He didn't approve of his unconscionable tactics, but he had a job to do by any means necessary.

"Do you have a taste for art, Detective?" Isabella asked as she entered the living room carrying a silver tray with servings of peach cobbler and coffee.

"I'm sorry, I didn't mean to be nosey."

"I understand," she said, cutting him off. "I expect people to be captivated by my collection because I designed it that way. However, I doubt you came all this way to praise me for my eclectic taste in art."

"You're right, I didn't," Donavan said taking a seat beside Sheldon. Isabella then lowered the tray allowing both Donavan and Sheldon to take their dessert and beverage. She then placed the tray on a nearby vacant and then took a seat across from the two men.

"Now, what else can I do for you gentlemen?"

"Actually, ma'am, we would appreciate it if we could speak to your client," Sheldon said, speaking for the first time since he entered and catching Isabella off guard. His words caused Donavan to grimace at him, but he had already committed to the statement and decided to finish it. "That is, in your presence, of course," he said spooning a healthy portion of cobbler into his mouth.

Donavan stood up and extended his hand to Melsean. "Good evening, Mr. Natas, I'm..."

"I know who you are, Detective Lynch. There's nothing wrong with my sense of hearing."

"Yes, well, we're sorry to disturb you two."

"I seriously doubt that, because if you were, you would have chosen a more appropriate time to discuss your plight."

"I can respect that, Mr. Natas. However, I can assure you that this will not take up too much of your time."

"Fine, then let me save you some by saying no, I did not kill Sergeant McCray, and yes, I was out at the time of the murder, but I was with a friend of mine named Andy Devilyn. She owns Andy Auto Service in Coney Island on Neptune. I don't have nor ever had a chain with an initial plate with the letters entwined in each other."

Donavan turned to Sherman with a puzzled expression as if silently questioning the deputy officer. Sherman shrugged his shoulders in response to his unspoken inquiry. Donavan faced Melsean again.

"Who told you we were investigating Sergeant McCray's murder and how did you know about the chain and name plate?"

"Duh—it was all over the news," Melsean said sarcastically.

"Okay, that explains the investigation, but what about the name plate? None of that information was released to the press?"

Melsean was about to respond when Isabella cut in patting him on the thigh as a sign to let her do her job.

"He got the information from me. How I got the information is my business."

"Ms. Danpier, you are aware that interfering with a police investigation is a criminal offense?"

"Yes, so is slander and noncompliance with the substantive laws governing your agency."

"I see," Donavan said averting his attention from Isabella and focusing again on Melsean. "So, what you're saying is it's a complete coincidence that it was your initials that wound up on that name plate?"

"Call it what you will, but like I said, I wasn't there, so you're beating a dead horse here."

Donavan put down his plate of barely-eaten cobbler and untouched coffee. "I guess that'll be all for now, but keep this in mind, as we speak, I have people lifting and dusting for prints. You'd better hope nothing comes up with your name on it. I'm going to be all over your ass like Michael Jackson on little boys at Neverland Ranch. Come on, Sheldon. We're done here."

Sheldon raised and handed the empty dishes to Isabella. "Thank you for the peach cobbler and coffee, Ms. Danpier. It was delicious."

"You're welcome, Officer Smith. Would you like some to take with you?"

Sherman was about to accept her offer when Detective Lynch yelled for him to follow him. "I'm afraid I'll have to take a rain check on that offer, but thanks nonetheless."

"No problem, Officer Smith. It was my pleasure," she said leading them to the door.

"Please call me Sherman, Ms. Danpier."

"Only if you call me Isabella."

"Sure. Isabella, that has a nice ring to it."

"Enjoy the rest of your night, Sherman," she said and Sherman responded by tipping his imaginary hat to her.

"I'll try, Isabella, and you do the same."

"Will do," she said, then looked at the detective with disgust as he said a flat good-bye and rolled his eyes without a backwards glance. Sherman left behind him, but stopped abruptly and turned around and to face Melsean.

"Good night, Mr. Natas."

"Likewise, Officer Smith. And get home safely."

Isabella shut the door behind them.

Donavan waited until he reached his car then swung around causing Sheldon to almost collide with him. "What the fuck was that about?"

"What was what about, Detective?"

"You know what I'm talking about! All that 'thank you for the peach cobbler and coffee, it was delicious, please call me Sherman, and the imaginary hat tipping bullshit!'"

"Well, it's true. It was delicious, and I prefer to be called Sherman."

"Yeah, well that's unfucking professional." Donavan got into the car and started the ignition. He didn't like being outsmarted, especially by a two-bit, hotshot lawyer that happened to be a woman. *I know it was that son-of-a-bitch,* he thought. *And I'm not going to rest until his ass is sitting in an asylum in New York State, awaiting his trip to the chair or chamber, even if it costs me my life.* He backed out of the driveway and sped off down the street.

Melsean stood at the window watching as the car lights faded into the night. He was worried about the outcome of this investigation. It was no secret that someone was going out of their way to frame him and assassinate his character. He couldn't help feeling that something bad and evil was in the making, and was going to leave a large trail of corpses in its wake as a message for him.

Isabella came up to him from behind, wrapped her arms around his chest, rested her face on the nape of his neck, and gently kissed him.

"Come to bed," she whispered, and Melsean allowed himself to be escorted to her bedroom where they made love till exhaustion overtook them. They slept in each other's arms, oblivious that tomorrow may be their last time together in the wake of their ancient nemesis.

Fifteen

*A*n intense migraine welcomed Desiree back to the land of the living with an overwhelming hangover. She rubbed her eyes and tried to blink out the sleep and sunlight that blinded her. It was 8:05 a.m. and she was supposed to have been at work thirty minutes ago. She knew she was going to get chewed out by her boss, but what's done was done. She'd call in as soon as she'd gotten up.

Desiree yawned and almost wretched from the sickening combination of orgasmic juices and shit that fouled her mouth. She didn't recall being fucked Greek, but what could she expect to remember as wasted as she was last night. She turned to the other side of her bed to find it empty with the exception of a letter that read:

Dear Lady,
Thanks for last night. I needed that, but I don't think it would be wise for this to go any further given the way things started between us. Then again, who

knows, we might meet again on a lonely night while full of hard liquor, until then...

Guess who?

"Kiss my ass, motherfucka!" she hissed, ripping the letter to shreds, then fanning the acrid odor of her breath away from her nose. *Apparently, I'm the one who was French kissing assholes last night from the smell of it,* she thought. Then no longer able to tolerate the odor, she got out of bed and went into her bathroom to get cleaned up.

Thirty minutes later, she was clean, dressed, and ready to leave. She made it her business to call her office and inform her boss that she was on her way, not to mention that she lied to the man, stating that she had car trouble and wanted to call sooner, but forgot to recharge the battery in her cell phone.

The head D.A. wasn't happy with her tardiness, but let her go with a warning to be more conscious of her priorities and surroundings. He admonished her for another minute before closing their conversation.

Desiree was on her way out the door when she remembered the fax Dr. Benning was supposed to send. She went into her study room and found the information she sought in the cradle. She folded it into her purse and proceeded to work. It took her a good hour and a half to get to Manhattan because of the congestion of the highway due to a car accident. Then, she had to search for a parking lot with a vacancy, which set her back another thirty minutes. The head district attorney unleashed a lecture on her about punctuality and obligation. Desiree squinted through it all as if such a thing could prevent her head from exploding from the loud talking.

When satisfied with his chastisement of his assistant D.A., Desiree was dismissed and sent to do some legwork for the office instead of her traditional court appearances, which took up the better part of the day. At around 3:30 p.m., she finally made it to her office to find that the fax sent to her at home was destroyed when it got jammed inside the machine. Luckily she had asked for a copy to be sent there at the office. Desiree didn't even think about what Dr. Benning had told her until now, and she still was having a hard time swallowing this information.

She read it at least three times before she made an attempt to phone Isabella. *I know the bitch is going to gloat about her being right,* she thought while dialing the number, *but given the circumstances, now is not the time to let my emotions supersede my intelligence.* Unfortunately, she kept getting a busy signal. "Come on, hang up the phone! This is important!" she barked into the receiver. Nothing seemed to be going right for her today. "Shit has been rolling down hill since I woke up this morning." All she asked for was for one thing to go right today and break up her streak of bad luck. What she was asking for seemed small in comparison to what others were pleading for. After everything she's been through, one brush of good luck for her would hardly be missed by any, if at all.

Desiree picked up the phone and dialed again,

this time it rang four times before someone picked it up revealing a masculine tone all too familiar to Desiree. Her voice became relieved and felt compelled to bear the truth. It appeared that her day was about to take a turn for the better. If only she knew that today would be her last experience with any kind of luck; both good and bad.

Sixteen

After Melsean and Isabella made love for the second time, he found himself overwhelmed with sleep and fell into a deep slumber. He was deep into his buried subconscious where there were no bars over time and space. He was taken back thirty years earlier to the time when he was to be born. His mother didn't believe in having children in hospitals. Only Melsean's father accompanied by a hired mid-wife, was allowed beyond the doors of her maternal agony.

It was sixteen torturous hours of labor before Eva delivered Melsean into this world. The older version of himself looked on motioning for somebody to enter the room. It was a young boy about the age of three. He looked familiar to Melsean, but he couldn't quite put his finger on why he knew him. What he did gather was that the boy was possibly related to them because he bore close resemblance to his parents. Melsean's father's name was Adam, and he led the child by his shoulders towards the bed where Melsean's mother lay spent, holding Melsean in her arms.

"Come and see you brother, Melsean," Eva said. "You're a big brother now. You have to protect him."

The young boy moved under the strength of his

father, closer to the bed. He stared at Baby Melsean as if he was a pariah or something because being so small was unheard of. All of a sudden, his face contorted and he hawk spit into Melsean's face as if his presence repulsed him.

"I hate you! I hate you!" the young boy raved as the midwife attempted to grab him only to be dodged by his quick movement. He reached into his pants and brandished a Swiss army knife and took a swing at Melsean's face. His mother was too weak to fend off the boy's advances and could only cry and shield Melsean from his assaults.

The grown up Melsean became agitated by what he'd seen and jumped in the way of the boy to block his path, but the boy went right through him, and with one swinging motion, slashed at Baby Melsean, but ended up cutting his mother. By then, his father grabbed him and dragged him from the room, kicking, scratching, and spitting his abominations towards Baby Melsean as the door closed behind them.

The picture then faded to black and zoomed in on another time and event. Melsean was now seven-years-old and was celebrating his birthday. All the kids from the neighborhood were invited and came bearing gifts for the occasion. Little Melsean was wearing a red and white OshKosh B'Gosh jumpsuit with a matching hat. In addition to that, he wore a red and white pair of Nike Delta Force sneakers that his mother bought him for his birthday.

The grown Melsean stood against the side of the house bewildered by all this. He couldn't recall

any of these events ever taking place. In fact, everything up until the age of seven was a blank. None of
this made sense to Melsean. His concentration was
broken by the sound of screeching tires causing
Melsean to turn abruptly. The young Melsean ran
past the big Melsean and made his way to the street.
Parked on the curb was a white sedan with the
words labeled *Saint Katherine's School of
Psychodynamic Studies for the Gifted.*

A priest emerged from the driver's side of the
car followed by a nun of some sort from the passenger side. The young Melsean ran to the car and
peered through the tinted windows as if expecting
someone. The priest rounded the vehicle and
stopped before Melsean and extended his hand as if
to shake it, but instead he lightly moved the boy out
of the way of the back passenger door and opened
it.

Little Melsean looked in as well as the grown
Melsean who was just as curious as this smaller version. Out of the back seat came an older version of
the boy that tried to slash Melsean as an infant, but
something appeared to be different about him. His
face showed no sign of emotion; only the blank stare
of a vacant shell that still possessed the ability to
vehicle its physiological functions.

Melsean's mother and father came out of the
front door to meet their son and thank the priest for
taking the time to bring him. The young Melsean
grabbed his older brother by the hand to lead him to
the backyard, but he wouldn't budge.

"Come on, Cain. Don't you wanna see what I

got for my birthday?" young Melsean asked.

Big Melsean moved in closer to the two in order to get a better look at what was happening. While the big Melsean stood there, his parents were totally oblivious to his presence, but one person noticed him. Cain seemed to focus on him directly. The big Melsean kneeled in front of his older brother and placed a finger in front of his face. He then began to move it left and right, and Cain's eyes followed.

"This can't be happening," the big Melsean said. "I'm dreaming. You can't possibly see me." He kept moving his finger and Cain's eyes followed it. Melsean turned to the younger him and used the same finger method on him, but he didn't respond. He brought his finger back to Cain's face and he responded, but this time his face contorted into a monstrous form, baring two rows of razor sharp teeth and bit the big Melsean's finger off.

"I felt that!" Melsean said, examining the stub where his finger used to be. "Holy shit, I felt that!"

He looked at the younger him, only to find that he was stuck frozen in the same arm tugging position, only Cain's arm was free from his grip. His mother and father were also frozen motionless, along with the priest and the nun. The only people, or things for that matter, moving were Melsean and Cain. Melsean tried to make a run for the priest's car, but was blocked by Cain. He rummaged around the area for something he could use for a weapon against Cain, but nothing littered the curb, lawn, or walkway. There was only one thing for Melsean to do and that was fight the monstrosity head on.

His first move was to psyche himself into see-ing Cain as the monster he was and not the little boy he appeared to be. Cain watched him closely, never taking his eyes off of Melsean, calculating his every breath, thought, and motion. Melsean, realizing Cain wasn't going to make the first move, balled his good hand into a fist and swung at Cain, but he caught Melsean's hand in his mouth and bit it off. Melsean screamed in agony as he cradled his nub between his arm and upper torso while attempting to run from Cain. He tried to run for the house, but was tripped by the younger Melsean who now became solid mass as the bigger Melsean fell and doubled on his back.

He looked from left to right as his parents, the priest, the nun, and little Melsean surrounded and loomed over him. Melsean stared at his parents' faces, noticing that they no longer had the softened qualities of love, but pure hate and ill will for him.

"Mom! Dad! It's me, Melsean. Don't you guys know me anymore?" he pleaded.

They ignored his pleas and chanted in one har-monizing voice, "It's lunchtime! Come and get it, Cain!" They then made a hole in their circle to allow Cain to enter inside.

Cain's shark-like teeth were still dripping blood as pieces of Melsean's flesh stuck to them like plaque. Cain looked down at Melsean, cracking a grin, and said, "I'm coming for you little brother, and this time I will have my blessings. For now, it's lunch time!" he said taking a deep chunk out of Melsean's neck.

Melsean jerked himself awake with his left hand still clenched under his right pit and his right hand holding his neck to stop the flow of blood. His chest heaved uncontrollably while he was sweating profusely all over his body. His head throbbed insatiably, pumping the blood through the gray matter of his mind.

"Melsean, wake up. It's lunchtime," Isabella yelled from the steps. "Come on! You're not going to sleep all day now, are you?"

Melsean sat there another few seconds before pulling his hand from its hiding to find that it was still intact. So was his neck, which was a comfort to him. He inhaled deeply and released it slowly as if to blow out all traces of his nightmare, but chances were slim of that happening and he knew it.

"Melsean, don't make me come up there and drag you down. Come and eat. I have to go to work soon and I want to make sure you eat something before I do."

Melsean, finally registering the reality of her voice, pulled the sheets to the side, slid off the bed, and made his way to the door. He opened it and elevated his voice enough for Isabella to hear him downstairs. "I'm up, Isabella. Give me a few minutes to brush my teeth and freshen up a bit. I'll be down shortly."

"Okay, I'll be in the dining room waiting."

He listened to the sound of her walking away. He didn't really feel like eating, given what he had just experienced in his dream, but he did feel hunger pangs in his stomach that needed tending to. He left

Isabella's room and went to retrieve his toiletries from his suitcase in the guest room then proceeded to wash up for lunch. Six minutes later, he was downstairs in a wine-colored satin pajama set by Kenneth Cole. Isabella stared at him as if seeing him for the first time. Melsean began to inspect himself from head to toe.

"Why are you looking at me like that? Is there something on me?"

"No, you're fine," Isabella said assumingly.

"Then why are you staring like I have egg on my face?"

"Well, to be totally honest with you, I was admiring your pajamas."

"My pajamas?"

"Yes, your pajamas. I couldn't see them last night being it was dark and all, but other than that, has it ever occurred to you that you just might happen to be a gorgeous man?"

"Actually it hasn't—go figure," he answered straight-faced and folded his arms.

She looked at him disbelievingly until he broke the silence with laughter. "Cut it out, Melsean. I'm being serious," she said, nudging him with her elbow.

"Okay. No, but seriously," he said, pasting a more sober-serious look on his face. "I wasn't what you would call a stud when I was growing up. I had a hard time expressing myself to females because I didn't feel I had anything to offer them."

Isabella shook her head to clear away some of her confusion. "Wait a minute. Let me get this straight. You mean to tell me that you were intimidated by girls?"

Melsean considered her question, even though it struck him as odd being he could've sworn he just answered it. "Well, yeah, you can say that."

She laughed uncontrollably, causing Melsean to become uneasy.

"That's rude. What's so funny about what I said?"

She raised and waved her hands as she tried to regain her composure. "You're right, I'm sorry. But you've got to admit that what you just said was some heavy stuff. I mean, my God, look at you, you're gorgeous,nice body with eyes that suck you into them. What female would possibly turn down someone like you unless she was either lesbian or retarded, and the dead don't count because the only thing they're turning down is a coffin and that's by the hands of the undertaker.

Melsean laughed at her. "You're a piece of work, you know that?"

"You think that's something, wait until you taste lunch. Come, let me show you." She led him by the hand into the dining room then escorted him to his seat. He was amazed at what he saw on the table. Isabella had made scrambled eggs with cheese, fried chicken, Belgian waffles, lightly dusted with powdered sugar and cinnamon, cream of wheat, and a punch bowl full of fresh fruit salad containing peaches, kiwi, guava, papaya, cherries, cantaloupe, and strips of fresh mango.

"Wow! Are we expecting more guests because I can't eat all of this?"

"No, Melsean, I'm not expecting any guests. I didn't know any particular food you might've liked for lunch, so I decided to give you a wide variety of choices. You like?"

"Do I? My mouth is watering, Bella."

"Bella?"

"Yeah, as in girl. Your name is kind of long, so I thought I'd shorten it up a bit—that is if you don't mind."

"Oh no, Bella's fine. It just caught me off guard, that's all. I haven't been called Bella since my father died."

"I'm sorry. I didn't know."

"Nonsense, how could you have known? Besides, it's been so many years since he's passed that I don't know how it makes me feel anymore. But never mind that, sit down and eat before the food gets cold."

"Yes, ma'am," Melsean said then began to eat.

The doorbell rang and Melsean rose from the table. "I'll get it."

"No," Isabella said, grabbing his arm as she got up from her seat. "You stay here and eat. I'll get the door." She proceeded to the door with her silk, lavender kimono trailing behind her. Melsean caught a glance of her G-string as she fixed her robe around her.

"Work it, baby! Work it!" he said, then growled like a tiger extending his hand in the gesture of a paw.

"Don't be fresh," she giggled and vanished around the bend.

Melsean couldn't believe how comfortable he felt around Isabella. It was almost unnatural the way they hit it off in a day's time. He did find her fascinating, but something was out there killing everyone close or associated with him. He heard Isabella laughing with a man's voice in the background. Jealousy began to well inside of him, but it was a quickly dismissed by his rational thinking. *Surely she wouldn't invite another man in when one is already present—I mean, not unless she's freaky like that.*

"Melsean, I want you to meet my best friend and co-worker at my firm. Kayman, meet Melsean. He's my client."

"It's a pleasure to meet you, Kayman," Melsean said, wiping his hands on the napkin then extending it to Kayman with a firm handshake. Something felt weird about it. It was as if he had done this before. "Forgive my forwardness, but have we met before?"

"Have you ever been in trouble before this time and needed an attorney?" Kayman asked.

"Truthfully, no."

"Then I don't see where our lives would have crossed. We're talking about two separate worlds here."

"You've got a good point there."

"Ah. I see I'm just in time for lunch and mmm..." he sniffed the air, "does it smell delicious."

"Well, since you're here, you might as well join us. There's more than enough as you can see."

"I don't have to be anywhere for a while, I guess I have time for a bite or two," he said, sitting while Isabella tucked his seat beneath him. "So, Melsean, what do you think of your attorney?"

"I think she's wonderful. I couldn't have chosen a better lawyer to assist me."

"Wonderful, huh? What makes her wonderful? You two have only met yesterday."

"Let's put it this way, Kayman, yesterday morning I was sitting in a hot, humid pen surrounded by human health hazards for a crime I didn't commit. Then all of a sudden, Bella stepped in and worked her mojo. So to me, she is wonderful and more. I will never forget that."

"Bella?" Kayman turned to Isabella and whispered.

"Yes, that's what he calls me."

"That's a bit personal for such a short time of meeting each other, don't you think?"

"No. What I do think is that it is for me to decide what I want to be called and by whom. You feel me?"

"Oh, indubitably. Point well noted. I didn't mean to offend you or cause you to spit fire," he said in between bites of chicken and waffles. "It's just the first time I heard someone call you Bella since your mother. Not to mention I wasn't the only man that I recall to ever shorten your name...until now that is."

"Look, I'm sorry if I said anything that might have been perceived as offensive."

"No, Melsean," Isabella interrupted. "You have no reason to be sorry. I!" she said poking herself in the chest, "was not offended by anything you said.

I happen to like it when you call me Bella, and I know Kayman can understand that, don't you, Kayman?" she glowered.

"Like I said before, point well noted. Now if we're done with that ordeal, I'd like to know how things went with the detective last night."

"Oh, the usual. He said he just came to ask a few questions in regard to last night's murder, but really he already had Melsean tried and convicted in his mind."

"You'd think he had something personal against me," Melsean cut in.

"Yeah, I know the feeling," Kayman said, looking at Isabella.

"I know you didn't just take a pot shot at me, Kayman?"

"Come on, Issey, you know that's not even my style."

"Yeah, well sometimes you like to slide your slick shit in for a good laugh."

"No, I don't."

She looked at him insistently.

"Okay, I do, but I'm being serious now. Don't expect Sergeant Lynch to fold his cards in the beginning of the hand. At least not without calling your bluff a few times."

"Don't worry..." she said smiling girlishly at Melsean, "I know his kind and it doesn't frighten me in the least."

Kayman looked from Isabella to Melsean and back. He had seen something, but held it in and smiled. "Well, I don't know about you two, but I'm stuffed." He rose from his chair. "I should be getting back to work with all of the depositions I have to get out of the way."

"Ah, come on, Kayman. You got more seniority in that firm than I do. You can stay out for weeks on end without making one phone call to explain your absence and they wouldn't bitch about it either."

"True, but I've already overstayed my welcome. Look, it's already one-thirty and I've got a long drive back to the office ahead of me."

"You know, I don't recall you ever meeting my friend April."

"No, but you told me about her."

"And I told her about you, but that isn't the same. I want all of my friends to know each other socially and not just through third-party messages."

"What if I stop by when I get off work? You can call her over again and we can hook up then. How about that?"

"I think it's a marvelous idea," Isabella said and threw her arms around Kayman's neck. She escorted him to the door and he left the dining area without so much as a sideway glance at Melsean. Neither did he speak to Isabella until they were by the door and out of Melsean's ear range. Kayman grabbed her by the elbow and brought her close to him.

"What was that all about back there?"

She looked at him puzzled. "Back where? What was 'what' all about?"

"Don't play naïve with me, Issey. I'm talking about those looks you and Melsean gave each other back there in the dining room."

"Oh, that—that was nothing. Just some harmless humor, that's all."

"Harmless, huh? That's not what it looked like to me."

Isabella became defensive and could no longer be civil about the issue. "I mean, so what if there was something going on between Melsean and I. What business is it of yours?"

"Issey, I'm your friend. I..."

She cut him off. "I don't appreciate your lip sermon. I am an adult. I pay my own bills. And I have no man. Where do you get off telling me what I can and cannot do?"

"Well excuse me, 'Ms. I'm-gonna-hook-you-up-with-my-girlfriend-April.' I guess I should be asking you the same."

"I was just trying to help you, Kayman. You're so self-absorbed at work that you never have time to find a friend. I just thought I'd lend you a hand."

"And I appreciate that. Really I do. But if you were truly paying attention, you'd see that the only woman my heart is ever going to beat for is you."

"We've already discussed this, Kayman, and I do not intend on going through it again with you. We're friends, nothing more. You need to learn to accept that."

Kayman brushed past Isabella down to the porch steps and turned around once he got to his car. "Accept what? That you never truly gave us a chance or the fact that you chose an accused killer over me? You are already fucking him and it hasn't been a full twenty-four hours yet? Oh, let's not forget the so-called friend you keep trying to force on me."

"Kayman, it's not even like that."

"It is like that, Issey! Only you can't see it or refuse to see it. But, I'll tell you this, I know what's best for me, so when I see someone taking what's supposed to be rightfully mine, excuse the fuck out of me because I can't just accept that!" Kayman got into his SL 500, started the ignition, and backed the car out of the driveway.

Melsean came to join Isabella on the porch to see if she needed some help after hearing some of what Kayman said. At first, he told himself that he would stay out of it, but by the tone of Kayman's voice, one would have to interpret it as getting out of hand. He stood in front of Isabella and immediately noticed that she was crying and he put his arms around her for comfort. He could see Kayman staring coldly at him for a minute before putting the car in drive and speeding towards the gate.

"What was that all about?" Melsean asked.

"Nothing, just a little history coming back to haunt me, that's all."

"Is there anything I can do to help?"

She considered what he asked and was unsure exactly how to respond. She decided to go with her heartfelt sentiment.

"As a matter of fact there is—keep making me feel the way I feel about you now and I'll be fine." She only hoped Kayman could find some peace of mind.

Seventeen

*D*etective Lynch entered the office well before his shift started. In his hand, he carried a box of cop's traditional pastime meal—a dozen of assorted pastries from Dunkin Donuts. He entered his office, closed the door behind him, and found a spot on his desk that would give him easy access to his cream-filled treats.

Donavan Lynch was like your average homicide detective. On his wall, he had various article clippings of every case solved and unsolved throughout the course of his career. He had no wife or progeny to carry on his legacy because he didn't have the time. Every waking hour was spent chasing the evils of society. His father was a captain in this precinct and had a hell of a score-card in arrests before he retired ten years ago. His pops was the one who encouraged him to follow his foot-steps when the rest of his friends were either in jail, dead, or running from the fate of either.

He was indecisive about it in the beginning, not

wanting to appear to others as a daddy's boy, so he found himself becoming socially despondent toward his father as an act of rebellion. He remained that way for about a year until the untimely murder of his father in the course of a strong-arm robbery. It would have never occurred had his father not been out late that night searching for him. Donavan immediately joined the New York Police Academy after the burial of his father. The men responsible for his father's death were never apprehended under those charges. Since that day, Donavan promised himself that unless he was on the verge of dying, he would spend not one single day relaxing until he found his father's killers.

Officer Davis and Smith rapped the door of Lynch's office and entered, taking a seat in front of his desk. Officer Davis looked at his watch.

"Aren't you a bit early for work, Detective?" Officer Davis asked

"That's funny, because I was going to ask you two the same question. What bring you gentlemen here to my humble abode?"

"Well, first of all, here's that report you asked for," he passed a set of papers to Detective Lynch. "Second, that initial plate we found yesterday at the crime scene, the crime lab was able to pull a couple of partial prints."

"That's good news, isn't it?" Donavan asked optimistically.

"Not quite," said Sheldon. "The prints that came off of the gold plate belonged to the victim, not the perp."

"So, basically we're back where we started."

"Again, not quite," Davis cut in. "We did find some traces of blood at the crime scene and it doesn't match the deceased."

Donavan looked back and forth between Davis and Smith, not knowing which one to address the next question to, so he decided it was best to talk between them. "Okay, that's good. Now we're getting somewhere. How long before we get the results?"

Davis and Smith looked at each other then spoke in sequence. "In a matter of hours."

"My God, what were you two doing, rehearsing this shit before ya'll came here?

"Sorry," they said together.

"Never mind that. Have a donut, fellas, and get comfortable because something tells me today is going to be a long one.

Eighteen

April arrived at Isabella's house at two-thirty sharp. She was wearing a powder-blue silk set by Vera Wang and a matching pair of two-inch sandals. Isabella always took a liking to her friend's fashionable taste. Everything fit her like a silicone glove. April perused the house, moving from one corner to the other.

"Girl, what's your problem?" Isabella asked, stepping in front of her.

"I'm looking for that hunk of a man you're hiding in here. Where is he?"

"Last time I checked, I owned this house, but maybe it was a typo or something, because you're gallivanting around like it belongs to you," Isabella said sarcastically. "And another thing, I don't want you smothering him. You feel me?"

"Come on, girlfriend. You know I don't mean any harm. It's not like you two are an item or anything."

Isabella turned away from April in silence triggering the obvious from April.

"Oh no, you didn't! You fucked him, didn't you?"

Isabella remained silent.

"Oh my God! You did fuck him."

"It's not like that, April, and keep your voice down."

"Why? Nobody's here to hear us, is there?"

"Yeah, Melsean."

"Listen, love, Melsean is a grown-ass man and I'm sure if he's been with other women, he knows they love to gossip."

"Is that what all those huddles and bathroom breaks are about?" Melsean said, sitting on the bottom flight of steps. Both women were startled by his presence and swung around to face him.

"How long were you sitting there?" April asked.

"Long enough to hear you tell the secret of the day." Melsean stood up and came off the last step toward Isabella and her friend. "And you must be Isabella's good friend April, right?"

"Wrong."

"Wrong? Who are you then?"

"I'm her best friend and she's mine," April said defensively.

"Okay, best friends—slip of the tongue. April, it's a pleasure to meet you." He extended his hand."

"Likewise, I'm sure," and she extended her hand and they formally greeted each other. "So, did you enjoy the cobbler?"

"Oh, the cobbler was excellent," Isabella

chimed. "It was by far one of the best dessert dishes I've had in a while."

April stared at her suspiciously. "Thanks, but I was talking to Melsean."

"It was definitely something new to my taste buds."

"So, you didn't like it?"

"I didn't say that."

"I didn't hear you deny it, either."

"Yes, April. I liked it."

"You really liked it? I mean you're not jut saying that to be nice are you?"

"No, sweetheart, but if I was, trust that my only reason for doing so would be that your feelings matter to me."

April blushed at Melsean's statement because nobody had ever said anything like that to her before, not even her ex-boyfriend Ramir. He wooed her with money, gifts and dick, but rarely did he fix his lips to form the three words every woman looked forward to hearing.

The father clock chimed three times indicating that it was three o'clock on the nose, which reminded Melsean where he was supposed to go.

"Ladies, I would love to continue our bonding session, but I have a previous engagement and I must keep my appointment."

Isabella was partially skeptical of Melsean's actions and decided to speak on it.

"April, can you excuse yourself for a minute? I need to talk to Melsean alone."

"Uh, I know what that means—lover's quarrel."

"April, please!" Isabella raved.

"Okay, okay. I'll be in the kitchen raiding the fridge if you need me."

Isabella waited for her to completely clear out before she focused her attention on Melsean, who had an astonished look on his face as he shook his head.

"I can't believe you just did that," Melsean said. "What's your problem?"

"My problem is that the last time you pulled a disappearing act someone connected to you turned up dead. The investigators were just here last night because of their suspicions and now you're leaving again."

"So, you think I'm guilty, too, huh?" he hissed.

Isabella had to rethink her strategy. Her conversation with Melsean was taking a turn for the worse and that was not her intention. She needed to get some form of control of the situation and ease the tension between them. "No, I'm just overreacting, but I can't help it. I'm concerned about you, Melsean, not just as an attorney, but more."

Melsean softened his composure. He felt ashamed for losing his cool and knew that sooner or later it would become his greatest downfall in life. The image of his so-called brother biting into his neck was framed in his mind, torturing his subconscious mind to the point it was now fighting its way to the surface.

"I want you to be more to me," Melsean stated sincerely. "I want us to be more to each other, but that's not going to happen if you don't learn to trust me."

"I understand, but you need to learn how to communicate with me and not get defensive every time I touch what you consider to be a sensitive spot."

"You're right. I need to work on that and I will, I promise. Truth is, I haven't felt like myself since the day Annette was murdered, and today was even worse."

"Today? What happened today?"

"I had a bad dream, actually two in the same day."

"Yeah? Tell me about it."

He told her the quick version of what he saw in his dreams and Isabella stood quiet as he went through it detail by detail. The clock chimed once to announce a half-hour had passed. Isabella heard the phone ring and was about to get it when she heard April in the kitchen.

"Y'all keep talking. I'll get it."

"Thanks, April," Isabella shouted, then returned her attention to Melsean. "What do you think it means?"

"I'm not sure, but I have a feeling I will soon. Listen, it's getting late and I have to meet Andy at her shop. She's going to store some of my things at her house."

"Will you be gone long?"

"I really can't say. I guess it would depend on traffic and the amount of haul."

"I'll have dinner waiting for you when you get in."

"You don't have to wait for me to get back, Bella."

"I know, but I want to. Having company beats dining alone any day, especially when it's someone you care about."

Melsean put his hands on both sides of her cheeks and pulled her close to him as her mouth opened to welcome his tongue. They kissed each other passionately as their hands explored hidden treasures, lingering on the most intimate places, expressing their nostalgia. Isabella felt her lava bubbling inside her, but remembered April was a few feet away in the kitchen.

"Perhaps you should leave now and we'll pick up where we left off tonight."

"Yeah, that would be best. I'll see you later." He gave her another long, wet kiss before exiting the house. Isabella stood frozen with her back leaned against the door holding her breath until she heard Melsean's car start and pull off down the road to the exit gate.

"Damn, girl! I can hear your pussy smacking all the way in the kitchen," April said entering the living room with a giant bowl of ice cream and Oreos. "The shit sounds like a tribe of Ethiopians at an all you can eat buffet."

"Shut up, bitch, and make sure you don't spill any of that food on my carpet," Isabella said as they laughed and went to watch a tape together. "Oh yeah, who was that on the phone for me?"

"Nothing to worry about. It was the wrong number," and nothing else was said on the matter.

Nineteen

Desiree Wilson paced back and forth in her office. It had been four hours since she spoke to Isabella about her findings and she couldn't understand what was keeping her. *Dammit, Isabella, where are you?* Desiree thought. *You said you'd be here two hours ago. What's keeping you?* Desiree didn't like being alone in the building, especially under these circumstances. It had been two hours since the District Attorney's office shut down for the day and she did not anticipate being there so long—at least that's what she told the night janitor, who told her to lock up behind herself.

She became more impatient by the minute and had run out of things to do to occupy time. It was 7:40 p.m. and she couldn't help but to think of all the places that she could be rather than in the office. *I've got better things to do than sit here waiting on her to show up when she feels like it! I'll give her five more minutes and*

I'm leaving. The better part of those five minutes was spent reviewing the lab reports she received last night. Nothing about that information made sense to her. It was utterly and biologically impossible for the reports to determine what they did. She spread them over her desk and began highlighting all of the important stuff.

As bad as she could use another win on her courtroom scorecard, she wasn't willing to do it at the expense of an innocent man, especially when the information was in her hands. There was no way she was going to intentionally send an innocent man to prison or death row when there were enough guilty souls eager to spend most or the rest of their natural lives behind bars.

Five minutes had passed and Desiree was ready to head home when the phone rang. At first, she was skeptic about answering it because of the hour of the day, but then she considered her reason for still being there, which was Isabella. She answered the phone.

"Hello, Isabella, is that you?"

Nobody responded.

"Hello?"

There still was no response. Desiree began to get worried and sensed danger at the other end of the phone line.

"Isabella, if that's you, quit playing around. I'm serious."

All of a sudden an all too familiar voice sounded through the phone, but it wasn't Isabella, nor anyone she'd considered a friend.

"And the Lord said listen to what the unfair judge says; and will not God procure justice for his own chosen, who laboreth day and night? I tell you, he will procure justice for them in short order."

"Who is this and what do you want?" the now terrified District Attorney asked.

The voice on the other end became a myriad of voices that growled deep into the phone.

"Your soul! We want your soul! Any objections?" They broke into a guffaw. "Don't mind coming outside to meet us. We're already here thanks to the good ol' janitor. Bless his soul, I mean rest his soul."

The phone instantly went dead. Desiree clicked the line and panicked while trying to dial for the police, but she couldn't get a dial tone. She clicked the receiver over and over again out of desperation.

"Fuck!" She slammed the phone against the desk in anger. She then reached for her Firestar 9 millimeter pistol that was velcroed to the inside of her desk, cocked it, and slowly stepped out of her office. The hallway was filled with doors leading to offices of fellow district attorneys and at the end of the hall were an elevator and a staircase several feet away. The staircase appeared to be open, and she knew going into a closed-in space like an elevator could definitely earn her an early death certificate, so she aimed for the staircase. She took a few steps and noticed her shoes made too much noise on the waxed textile floor, so she removed them and began creeping down the hall one step at a time.

When she almost reached ten feet away, the elevator stopped on her floor, but didn't open. Desiree's heart skipped a few beats before resuming its normal functions. She stared with one foot poised in midair as she waited for the doors to the elevator to open, but they didn't. She knew it couldn't have gotten there on its own. Someone had to have sent it and she most definitely didn't want to find out who did. Desiree knew she couldn't stand around waiting for whoever was on the phone to come and get her, so she decided to get her ass to that elevator and get the fuck out of the building.

She took a long breath then lowered her foot to the floor. Her next task was putting some mobility into her legs, so she took one step, but nothing happened. She took another and another until she was less then a few feet away from the stairwell and stopped. *This is too easy*, she thought as her D.A. instincts began kicking in along with her will to survive. *If I was a killer, how would I finesse this scenario? Why is he allowing me to get to the stairs and why hasn't he jumped out of the elevator yet? He wants me to take the staircase so that I'll be trapped, but I've got a trick for him.*

She walked the last couple of feet, but instead of going to the staircase, she detoured to the elevator and pressed the button and ran inside. She pressed the lobby button and it automatically closed and began to drop. It only took less than twenty-five seconds to reach the bottom floor. The door opened revealing another long hallway before she could reach the exit. Desiree could taste freedom at the end of the hall and so far nothing popped out to get her. She walked out of the elevator and quietly walked, turning every now and then to see if anyone was behind her. When she got halfway down the hall, it dawned on her that she had left the lab reports upstairs; they were her main purpose for being there in the first place. She figured she'd wait until tomorrow when the building was more occupied. Then again, tomorrow was a weekend, so basically she was ass out.

Suddenly, the elevator doors shut, causing her to turn around, but still she saw nothing. She turned back around to face the door and was confronted by the silhouette of the janitor sweeping the floor by the front entrance.

"Leslie, is that you?" she asked, squinting her eyes to attempt to get a better look at him. "Leslie?"

The silhouette figure raised his hand and lightly waved it in a gesture of friendship.

"Leslie, it is you! Thank God," she said as she quickened her pace to get closer. "I thought something happened to you. There was this strange man on the phone and he implied that you were dead, but I knew he was lying."

At that moment, the janitor's dead corpse dropped to the floor exposing a giant monstrosity that couldn't possibly have hidden behind Leslie's small frame. It stood less than ten feet away from Desiree with its chest heaving in rage as it stared her down. She couldn't see much on the creature, but what little she did, made her almost lose control of her bladder. The monstrosity spoke in the most hideous voice that sounded as if hundreds were speaking at the same time.

"We've just met and already I'm a liar? I guess seeing is believing." It lifted the janitor's lifeless corpse, plunged its claws inside of him, and pulled from it his heart and brought it close to his face. "You see it just rips my heart out to hear you thinking of me in such a negative way."

That was all Desiree needed to see or hear. She spun on her heels and bolted up the hallway toward the elevator, but the indicator revealed that it was on the third floor. She detoured to the staircase and tried the knob but it wouldn't turn. Looking behind her, she found the creature taking slow, measured steps toward her. He was still about thirty feet away. Desiree ran back to the elevator and began to press for it. She looked behind her to find the creature gaining fast. He was now only fifteen feet away.

"Why run, Desiree?" he said in his gravel-like voices. "The outcome won't change. I have all night to make you suffer."

"Why are you doing this to me? I haven't done anything to you."

He began to speak in that familiar voice to her. "Quite the contrary, Ms. Wilson. You've done enough and I can't allow you to foil my plans."

"Oh my God, it's you! But the tests said..."

"And they were right, but that's another story in itself. I'm sure you're more interested in getting a nice helping of suffering and I intend to oblige."

He was only nine feet away. Desiree turned back to the elevator and beat on the button as if that was going to motivate it to hurry down.

"Is it true that D.A. not only means District Attorney by Devil's Advocate?" the creature asked offhandedly. "If so, then I'm sure you'll have no problem receiving employment where you're about to go."

Desiree banged the button on the elevator, pleading with it to open while keeping one eye focused on the beast as it neared her. She was about to faint when the doors opened and swallowed her in, shutting behind her. *Thank God for this messed up elevator!* she thought. *I'll never use another stairwell as long as I live!*

The creature beat against the elevator door as if it had no knowledge of the concept of pressing the button to open the doors. Desiree cowered to the rear of the elevator in fear that the creature would soon get in. Her only chance was to get back to her office, find the lab results, and get them to Isabella. She needed to know the truth, and if Desiree was going to die today, she didn't want to leave without doing at least one good deed for someone, and it might as well be her courtroom rival.

The creature stopped rapping on the door and attempted to rationalize with Desiree. "Come on, Desiree, let's not make this more difficult than it has to be. You're tired, and I smell it all over you. May I have the honor of permanently putting you to sleep like a dog?"

"Leave me the hell alone, and go back to hell

where you came from!" Desiree screamed.

"Sorry, been there, done that. By the way, your father Lawrence sends his regards, and told me to tell you to dress cool for your funeral because Arizona's got nothing on the place downstairs," he chuckled.

How did he know my father's name? she wondered but knew the obvious. *What he was saying has to be true because how else would he have known?* She decided to test him.

"If you really saw my father, then I'm sure he told you something personal that only he would know about me. That's all the proof I need that you've spoken to him."

"Interestingly enough, he told me you were a feisty broad and wouldn't settle for anything less than a well kept secret shared by you and him. But it wasn't actually all that kept, was it, Desiree?"

"What is that supposed to mean?"

"It means I don't blame your mother for walking out on your father or abandoning you. You would've done the same thing if you were married and caught your husband with your daughter in the most uncompromising position—especially if she was enjoying it and rooting him on."

Desiree went numb. Her mouth became dry as she took in what the creature said to her.

"How...how did you find...who have you been talking to?"

"Let me put it this way, your father and me dodged coal from the same bed of fire."

"You're lying!" she screamed, shaking her

head disbelievingly. "My father was a good man."

"I'm sure he was once upon a time," he said snidely. "Just like you were, but that was then and this is now. Have I satisfied your curiosity with my honest answers? If so, let's skip the cat and mouse chase and let Hell have its way, Desiree, or else this is going to be a very painful experience for you."

He's going to kill me regardless of what I do, she thought. *So why make it easy for him.* She pressed her office floor number and the elevator began to rise.

"Have it your way, mousey, but trust me when I say this is going to hurt you more than it's going to hurt me. Let the hunt begin."

Desiree dug into her pantsuit pocket and pulled out her palm pilot to look up Isabella's faxing information. She had to send her a copy of the lab reports and hope she had the resources to bring that creature down and send him back where he came from for good. From below, she heard banging noises followed by a steel-grinding break that had to be the staircase in the lobby. The elevator stopped on the thirteenth floor and opened revealing the same hallway Desiree recently walked down. She had to get to her office, but the first thing she did was peep into the stairwell.

"Desiree is that you? I don't see you, but I sure can smell you. Mmm mmm, I could just eat you alive. You'd like that, wouldn't you?"

Desiree closed the door as quickly as possible. She wasn't trying to stick around and shoot cheap dialogue with him while he made his way up the stairs, instead she ran down the hallway until she came to her office. She ran inside slamming the door behind her and locked it shut. She pushed her desk against it in hopes that it would keep the demon out. Desiree's mind wandered on Leslie the janitor. She felt it was her own fault that he was murdered. Had she not been so eager to share the information she found, Leslie wouldn't be lying in a pool of blood with a hole where his heart used to be. She grabbed the fax machine from off the desk, and placed it on the floor under it to keep her intentions out of the creature's view. She looked up to find no one there, then focused her attention back to the fax and installed the paper as she dialed Isabella's machine.

She looked up at the door again and nothing stirred from the other side. The fax was almost complete, but she had no clue as to what she was going to do about getting out of the place once she was finished. After her fax was completed, an old saying came to mind; *never put all of your eggs in one basket.* She immediately turned on her Gateway computer and printer. She logged on to the One Police Plaza website and placed and email copy of the report to be given to Detective Donavan Lynch. She then pressed enter and watched as the machine indicated its task completed.

Desiree felt some form of relief from successfully sending off her information to both parties. Her only concern now was to find a way out of the building without the creature getting to her. She knew she couldn't possibly leave by way of using the front door. She needed something more inconspicuous-

something he wouldn't expect like the window. She looked out only to find the creature crouched at the window waving at her with a look of glower on his face as he smashed in the window.

"Sorry to keep you waiting..." he said jumping into the room, "but I do love to make a smashing entrance."

Desiree turned on her heels and was about to attempt to remove the desk from her path when the creature leaped on top of the desk to hinder her progress.

"Enough running, already. Don't you see there is no escaping me? You made it this far because I allowed you to.

"Really, and I suppose you're going to share with me why?"

"Of course, it's quite simple. Actually I needed to know where you put those reports."

"What reports? I have no reports."

"I see," he said stepping down from the desk with muscles bulging through the spiked bones that covered his flesh. "I believe this is where we plea bargain, right?"

"You can say that. What do you have to offer?"

He reached out, grabbed her, and spun her to the desk, pinning her under his weight, "I understand why you're such a hard-on, Desiree."

"Yeah, and why's that?"

"Because you haven't had one in you in a long time, but all that is going to change tonight." He unzipped his pants and reached into his boxers causing Desiree to chuckle at him.

"And just what do you propose to do, fuck me to death?"

"You know, that's what I'm going to miss about you, Desiree," he said whipping out his engorged member encrusted with quarter-inch spikes on it. "Your crystal, clear perception of the obvious."

"No!" she screamed, fighting against his restraint to no avail. "Please don't! I'm begging you!"

"Ahh, come on. Don't tell me this is your first time because I've heard stories about you in your prime. You were Daddy's little cock slut, right? Oh, I know how you like it—trust me, this will be one hell of a ride." He slammed her on the desk then plunged his spiked dick through her pants and into her, knocking the wind out of her as he ripped at her insides.

"Oh my God! Wait! Wait! Take it out and I'll give you what you're looking for," she said in between pants. Her vaginal muscles tightened around his spiked phallus.

The creature leaned to his right, causing some of his spikes to plunge inside of Desiree's tender flesh and the sharp pains tortured her vaginal walls. He reached into her scanner and pulled out the set of papers he was looking for.

"Do you mean these? I knew they were there all the time."

"Then what is it that you want from me?" she asked, fearing the answer.

He leaned forward, this time causing her to

wince in pain until he was level with her ear. "I want to hear you scream!" He then shoved the remaining length of himself inside and fucked her corpse all the way to a screaming climax.

Twenty

*M*elsean didn't return to Isabella's house until nine o'clock that evening. He was speechless and appeared to be upset about something, but Isabella's interest lied somewhere else for the moment."

"So, how did the moving go? Did Andy have enough room for all of your stuff?"

"We didn't move anything. She wasn't home."

"Oh, so where have you been?"

"Driving around, thinking," he said absently.

"Do you have any idea what time it is, Melsean? You could have at least given me the heads up on what you were doing?"

"You're right, but I have a lot on my mind and it's troubling me."

"Really, come sit with me in the living room and we'll discuss it."

They walked into the living room and sat on the couch in front of the television. Isabella grabbed the remote and lowered the volume then turned her attention back to Melsean. "Okay, now tell me what's bothering you?"

Melsean took a deep breath then began from the beginning. "All right. Like I said earlier, I was going to Andy's so she could help me move some of my things to her house, but when I showed up, she wasn't there, nor could I find anybody that worked for her."

"Maybe they were out on break."

"Nah, no auto shop allows everyone to go on break at the same time. It's bad for business. Besides, I waited for like an hour and a half for her to show up, but no one did."

"I'm sure there's a logical explanation for it."

Isabella caught a glimpse of a special news bulletin and she raised the volume on the TV.

"This is Jasmine Diaco reporting for Channel 21 news. We're sad to report that in a horrid display of events, Assistant District Attorney, Desiree Wilson for the Kings County court division, was found earlier this evening, dead from internal hemorrhaging after being brutally raped and sodomized with a suspected serrated knife. So far, there have been no arrests, but stay tuned and we'll bring you more as this case progresses. This is Jasmine Diaco for the Channel 21 news at ten. Back to you, Penelope."

"See what I mean? Something is definitely wrong here," Melsean frowned.

"There's definitely an explanation for this," she said reiterating her previous response, "but I'm not sure we're going to like it. This does not look good, but it's still recoverable," she said, still attempting to offer hope, if not for his benefit, her own.

"Well, it gets worse. After I got tired of waiting for Andy, I decided to take a trip to my office and thank my boss personally for putting up all that money to hire you. He told me he didn't know what I was talking about."

"What?"

"I'm serious, Bella."

"That's absurd. I was paid a check to immediately start your case."

"I'm sure you were, but it didn't come from the company I work for."

Isabella sat dumbfounded. Nothing seemed practical anymore.

Melsean understood what she was going through and he knew something had to be done before somebody else wound up getting hurt. "Listen, would you happen to still have a copy of that check?" he asked.

"Yeah, why?"

"Because somebody's John Hancock has to be on it if you cashed it."

Isabella's eyes brightened with comprehension of Melsean's point. "I see your vision. I'll be back in a minute." She ran off to retrieve it.

Melsean thought about the nightmare he had yesterday. It weighed heavy on his mind and made its way to his consciousness, invading his privacy even while awake. He knew there was hidden significance between what was going on and he feared before it got better it would get worse—much, much worse.

Twenty-One

*D*etective Lynch stood in the office of District Attorney Desiree Wilson's, staring at her lifeless body as it lay on her desk. Her legs were cocked all the way back with her feet tucked behind her head in a forced double-jointed effort and strips of flesh hung from her vagina as if somebody had placed hooks inside of her and ripped her insides out.

Officer Sheldon Smith had been helped out of the office after puking on the crime scene. Donavan had him removed as to prevent him from further contaminating the crime scene. Thirty minutes later, Sheldon was allowed back in with the promise that he would stomach it without further incident. He stared down at Desiree and trembled from the permanent look of fright on her face. He wondered what she could have possibly seen to cause her face to contort in such a fashion.

"Jesus Christ, who could've done such a thing?" Sheldon asked.

"Only two I know and Jeffrey Dahmer has been dead for years. That leaves Melsean Natas as the perpetrator."

"What makes you think it was him?"

"Because it has his signature all over it. So far, everybody associated with his case has found a one-way ticket to the medical examiner's office."

"What are we going to do now?"

"The only thing we can do right now is re-arrest Mr. Natas and bring some serenity back to these mean streets because he's no longer satisfied with killing average tax payers. He's after those of official capacity."

"I think we should honestly rethink this whole investigation thing. The whole setup here is too simply placed and I don't see Mr. Natas as a careless crook."

Detective Lynch gave Officer Davis a once-over then spit venom at the man. "Who the fuck asked you what you think and what's this *we* stuff about? I don't recall the commissioner calling you in because you have a PHD in psychology and understand the psychosis of a killer, or else I wouldn't be here."

Officer Davis disregarded the man's vehemence because he knew he was only being a prick because he was stressed over the political pressures of the case. "Listen, Detective, I understand your plight and I honestly wish to help you here..."

"Do you really want to help me?"

"Yes, I do."

"So, you really, really want to help me?"

"I said I do."

"Then shut the fuck up and let me do the job they pay me to do!"

"Okay, have it your way. Just consider me background."

"Very good, Background," Lynch said sarcastically. "Now let's go get our killer."

Twenty-Two

Isabella walked into her home office and went to her cherry wood desk to look for the copy of the check. When she got close to the desk, she noticed that somebody had faxed her some papers. She pulled them from the cradle and examined their contents.

On the left corner of the paper was a squared off line that read *To D.A. Wilson from the New York City Specimens Laboratory in Manhattan.* Isabella checked the top of the first page for a letter leading and found it with a number to be reached twenty-four hours a day. She dialed the number and asked for Dr. Troy Benning. There was a brief pause over the phone before Dr. Benning's voice came over the speaker.

"Hello, this is Dr. Troy Benning for the New York City Specimens Laboratory. How can I help you?"

"Good evening, Dr. Benning. My name is Isabella Danpier and I'm the defense lawyer for Mr. Melsean Natas."

"I see."

"Anyway, I just entered my home office and found a copy of a lab report sent to District Attorney Desiree Wilson in my fax machine. I was wondering if you had any idea why?"

"As a matter of fact, I do. I did a complete blood and DNA sampling on your client to see if he in fact was at the scene of the crime. I even went as far as hair and nail follicle matching along with a fingerprint sketch to ensure accuracy in the results."

"From what I see on this page, one could infer that the reports indicate my client as the killer, right?"

"Not quite that simple, Mrs. Danpier."

"It's Ms., and call me Isabella, please. Now what do you mean by 'not quite'?"

"Okay, Isabella, what I'm saying is we're dealing with a case of the same event that occurred in the city Nicea in the year 325 C.E, which means Common Era, over the issue of Arianism and to settle the dispute over Christ's divinity Homousious.

Isabella removed the phone from her ear, shook her head in confusion, and returned the phone to her ear. "I'm sorry, but I flunked esoteric literature and religious studies. You're going to have to be more specific."

Dr. Benning sighed in the phone, but could no longer hold his composure. "What the hell is wrong with you people? Don't you study anything? My God, it wouldn't hurt you to pick up a book on historical events sometime and put something substantial into your prehistoric minds. I swear legal beagles are intellectually lazy."

Isabella listened to him ramble on, raving about how people like her were suffering from a Rectal Cranial Inversion; she didn't know what that meant nor did she want to.

"I hope you're finished venting, Dr. Benning, because I'd seriously like to know what the Hobooreos mean."

"Sorry, I didn't mean to go tirade on you. I just wish somebody that calls for information would have at least a little knowledge on what I'm saying. The word is Homousios."

"Right, I'll make sure I prep myself before our next chat, I promise. Right now, I need that information."

"Homousios is a Latin word they used in Rome to describe Jesus Christ's divinity meaning 'of the same substance' that God is made of. However, in this case, we're dealing with Homoisios."

"And what's that, of similar substance or something?"

"Exactly," he said excitedly. His energy scared the hell out of Isabella. "I knew you had some cells left in that marijuana-fried brain of yours."

"Thanks a lot. I think."

"Your client seems to be involved in the same apparent scenario."

"So, what are you saying, that the DNA found at the crime scene is not from my client Melsean Natas, but somebody with strong similarities?"

"Something like that, only this person matches your client down to the genetic strand."

"Oh my goodness! I didn't know that was possible."

"Neither did I, and I've been studying genetic science practically all my life."

"Dr. Benning, you've been most helpful. I may have a couple more questions for you later."

"Feel free to call. Today I'm pulling an all-nighter, so give me a ring if you need me."

Isabella couldn't believe what she heard. The fact that there was somebody out there who was exactly like Melsean both mentally and physically really scared her. She had to tell him about this huge find, but she feared the way he would handle it.

She went back to the living room where Melsean was sprawled on the couch, listening to the breaking stories on the DA's murder. Isabella desperately wanted to run over to the couch and rip his feet from off of her cream leather couch, but figured with what she was about to tell him that he needed as much comfort as possible. She picked up the remote and clicked the TV off and sat on the coffee table in front of him.

"Hey, I was watching that."

"I know, but I have something important to tell you and I need your undivided attention." She grabbed hold of his hands into hers.

Melsean saw the seriousness in her eyes and immediately became worried. "Bella, what's the matter? Are you okay?"

"I was fine, Melsean, until what I just learned."

"Tell me. I need to know," he said searching her eyes.

Isabella told him about how she went to the room to get the copy of the check and noticed some papers in her fax machine's cradle sent by the deceased District Attorney. She told him about the results of the report, showing him the paper as she explained, and how she called the doctor from the lab that sent the report. She then shared the information about the Homousios and Homoisios. She watched Melsean's expression as she explained the occurrences of his problems leading up to now, and could tell that the information was hard for him to swallow. She could understand that because she wasn't quite sure she believed it, even as she sat there giving him the rundown.

"I know all this is a bit much to take in at one time and I know it sounds crazy."

"Actually, it doesn't."

"No, why's that?" she asked suspiciously.

He went through the motion of explaining his nightmare he had the other night in more detail about having a brother and how he was taken away to some kind of hospital.

"Do you think it was a real memory...something you repressed since your childhood?"

"I honestly don't know, but I intend to find out."

"Maybe we should share this information with the authorities and they can probably assist us better in this investigation."

Melsean laughed hysterically. "Please, picture Detective Lynch and his dupe of a deputy, Officer Smith, helping to clear my name. The man is too pragmatic to be any good to me."

"Well, in that case, we'd better be going because something tells me if you're right, him and his goons are on their way as we speak. Go get whatever you need and meet me at my truck."

"Why we got to take your vehicle? Mine has just as much traction as yours."

"True, but my Range Rover is dependable and safe, not to mention it rides corners like rails."

Melsean shook his head. "Fine, we'll take your rolling battle station. Now let's get what we're going to get and get to going."

They both picked out what they thought would be essential for their mission and met outside of Isabella's SUV. She unlocked her side of the vehicle then hit the switch to let him in. When he got inside and shut the door, Isabella reached into her coach bag and pulled out a Lorcin C.S. 9 millimeter pistol and passed it to Melsean. He looked at it like it was the most foreign thing he had ever seen.

"Hmm, what is this for?"

"It's called a gun and it's used to shoot, wound, and kill living things. It doesn't have a hammer so you have to be careful of the firing pin."

"I know that much, but why do I need it?"

"Because whoever killed your girlfriend, Sergeant McCray, and Desiree is making you look guilty. My advice to you is to make a citizen's arrest and clear your name."

Melsean thought about what she said. "You know that's not such a bad idea."

"I know, isn't this exciting?" she said, clapping

her hands and advancing in her seat. "So, what's our first move going to be?"

"Well, my guess is that whatever we're looking for we'll find the answers at Saint Katherine's School of Psycho Dynamics for the Gifted. Matter of fact, let me do the driving." Melsean hopped out of the jeep, circled around the front passing Isabella, and hopped into the driver's seat as Isabella closed the passenger side door. He turned over the engine, hitting the switch for the headlights, and placed the jeep in reverse. When he reached the end of the driveway, he cut the wheel, placing the car on the clear path to the gated exit and put the car into drive. Melsean waited until they were past the security gate and on the road before he said another word to Isabella.

"Bella, does your car phone work?"

"Of course, it works. Why?"

"I need you to dial information and get me the number and address for Saint Katherine's," he said as he merged onto a major highway leading southwest on I-95.

Melsean was so preoccupied with getting through the gate of Isabella's home that he never saw the black sedan parked along the side of the road. It started its engine and followed ten car lengths behind them as they sped down the road and merged onto the southern parkway.

Twenty-Three

*D*etective Lynch was told by the guard in the booth that they missed Isabella and her client by twenty-five minutes and he had no idea when they would be back. This upset the detective and he blamed Officer Davis for missing them. Had it not been for his constant questioning him and Sheldon, they would have been there earlier.

He asked the guard if he had any idea where they might have went but he knew nothing about their night excursion. Detective Lynch eventually managed to convince the guard to allow him to peruse her living quarters with the promise not to move or take anything from it. Donavan's only objective there was to find something that would give them a relatively good idea of where Isabella and her client were headed.

Donavan flicked on the lights and ordered Sheldon to check the rooms upstairs while he searched the bottom. The kitchen was clear and so was the downstairs bathroom. He went into Isabella's home office and began moving books around, searching for any hints that would suggest their next move. He moved to her desk and began rummaging there, stopping at her fax machine. He noticed something was

recently faxed, so he checked the screen which indicated that the number of the sender belonged to
the murdered district attorney.

Donavan checked the cradle of the fax
machine, but could not find anything that would con-
nect Isabella to the D.A. He then picked up the
phone and pressed redial. After two rings, a soft-
spoken gentleman with an English accent came on
the line.

"This is Dr. Troy Benning for the New York
Specimen's Laboratory. How may I serve you?"

"Good evening, Dr. Troy. This is Detective
Donavan Lynch from the New York City Homicide
Division and I was wondering if a woman by the name
of Isabella Danpier call you?"

"Yes, as a matter of fact she did."

"Good. I am investigating the murder of
District Attorney Desiree Wilson and..."

"Desiree Wilson, you say?" he cut in. "You
can't be serious."

Donavan leaned back in the chair. "Oh, but I
am, Dr. Benning. That's why I need your help, so I
can find the ones who did this to her."

"You're not suggesting that Ms. Danpier had
anything to do with it, are you?"

"I'm not saying anybody did anything. I just
need to know what she knows, so I can get a heads
up on solving this case."

"Well, like I said before, are you suggesting
that Ms. Danpier had anything to do with it, because
I can see how she would? After all, Ms. Wilson faxed
her a copy of the lab reports I sent her."

Donavan sat forward again and cleared his throat. "Lab reports? Explain to me what the alleged reports consisted of."

Dr. Benning spent several minutes explaining the theory of Homousios and Homoisious to Detective Lynch, including ostracizing him for his ignorance and berating his plans to combat intellectual laziness in America before hanging up.

Donavan felt his whole world crashing around him. He was so bent on sending someone down that it never occurred to him that he might be wrong. He looked almost toward the edge of the desk and noticed a manila folder which read *confidential*. Donavan looked inside and found a copy of a check for 2.7 million dollars, but what made it strange was the signer of the check—there was no printed name, only the chicken scratch signature of a left-handed person, judging by his penmanship. The only letters that could be distinguished were the beginning letters of the person's first and last name, *K* and *N*, next to the name and address of Saint Katherine's School of Psychodynamic Studies for the Gifted.

Donavan folded the paper and left the office after turning off the light and sliding the door behind him. He met up with Sheldon in the living room, who reported that he couldn't find anything of use. Donavan told him not to worry because he thinks he had a good idea where they were headed. He then motioned Sheldon to turn everything off and put everything back the way it was before they left. They then headed for Saint Katherine's.

Twenty-Four

*M*elsean turned off the southern parkway onto the Belt parkway heading south over the Verrazano Bridge. Every now and then, he would cut his eye at Isabella as she stared blankly out the window as the wind whipped her hair into her face. Melsean reached over and pulled the hair away with his pinky and decided to break the cold silence between them.

"I appreciate your wanting to help me, Bella. But you do know that you don't have to, right? I mean, I'll understand."

Isabella turned to face him and cracked a smile. "I'm sure you would, Melsean, but it was my choice to help you and I'm not going anywhere until I do just that."

Melsean admired her bravery and loyalty on a personal and professional level. She put everyone's needs ahead of her own and placed no high demands in return.

"You do know this can get dangerous? I'm not trying to scare you, but truth is I'm terrified about what I've seen in my nightmares and if he's the grown version of anything I've seen, you and me have plenty to worry about.

"I'm not afraid. I know you'll protect me."

"Who me? Please, I'm a punk."

"Who are you kidding? Nobody with guns the size of yours could possibly be a punk," she said squeezing his right arm.

"I am kind of big, aren't I?"

"Everywhere it counts, at least," she said as she moved her hand down to his swollen member and gave it a good squeeze causing Melsean to momentarily lose control of the vehicle.

"Don't do that," he said, steadying the wheel. "I'd like to get where we're going in one piece."

Isabella removed her hand and pouted her lips in a childish manner. "I'm sorry, Melsean, but I thought you could hold your own with a little road play."

"I can," he said turning to smirk at her. "It's when somebody else holds me that makes it a problem."

They went over the Verrazano and fifteen minutes later crossed the outer bridge taking it to the New Jersey Turnpike and picking up Interstate 13-South to Pennsylvania. Melsean and Isabella talked and laughed while listening to 98.7 Kiss FM's Quiet Storm hour. Melsean signaled his left turn signal to pass another vehicle and noticed a black Cadillac signaled the same, but had no reason to do it. He didn't give the Cadillac a second thought.

"We're going to have to stop for gas soon and fill up this tank because there's nothing worse than being stranded on a dark road."

"Actually there is," Isabella interjected. "Being stranded on a dark road when the authorities got an

A.P.B out on you is worse than that."

"Point well made."

Melsean saw a sign indicating a service area and rest stop two miles ahead and instead of waiting a couple of feet before the exit, he signaled the right turn-off well before a mile and a half. He noticed the same black Cadillac signaled his lights to turn off in the same direction.

"I believe we have company," Melsean said, staring in the rearview.

"Where?" Isabella asked, turning around in her seat.

"What are you doing?" Melsean asked, intercepting her before she could make a complete turn. "Don't do that. It's too obvious."

"But I want to see," she said with a twinge of frustration.

"Then look out your side view at the car with its right signal blinking."

Isabella looked out the window and noticed the black Cadillac with its right signal blinking in sequence with Melsean's.

"What are we going to do?" she asked, trying to hide her obvious anxiety.

"The only thing we can do, take care of the problem." He pulled out the gun, ejected the clip to make sure it was loaded, then inserted it again and cocked it.

Melsean pulled off the highway and into the exit lane, turning quickly around the bend and parked the Range Rover beside an eighteen-wheeler and cut off the engine. He then grabbed the gun off his lap and got out of the car.

"What am I supposed to do if he comes by the car?" Isabella asked.

"Just act normal, and shut the door."

Act normal? she asked herself. *How the fuck am I supposed to act normal at a time like this?*

Melsean stood behind the rig and watched as the black Cadillac crept off the exit and appeared to be searching for their vehicle. The car turned right and headed in their direction. Melsean hid behind the truck as the black sedan stopped a couple feet past the Range Rover and parked.

A young, burly man of dark hue stepped out of the car and began walking toward their vehicle. Melsean crept around the side of the truck as the man neared the passenger side door.

Isabella watched through the tinted window as the gruesome figure approached closer and closer. *Where the hell are you, Melsean?* she wondered as she ducked in her seat. A couple of seconds later, the man was up on her window looking in. At first he didn't see her, but then she made a sudden move that caught his eye and he tapped on the window.

"All right, I see you, so you might as well open up. Come on now, we don't have all night."

Isabella lowered her window and peeped at the gentleman. "What the hell's going on and why are you banging on my window?"

He pulled out a .40 caliber pistol and let it hang by his waist, but Isabella had already seen the light dancing off of it.

"Let's not play games, Missy. I know you know

why I'm here, so let's skip the melodramatics, shall we? I know he's here."

"Who's here? What are you talking about?"

The man began to raise his hand with the pistol in it. "That wasn't the answer I was expecting to hear. I know he's here with you. Somebody had to drive if you're in the passenger side. Where is Melsean?"

"Right behind you," Melsean said, placing the pistol to the man's head.

"Relax, okay. You don't want to do this, son."

"You're right. I don't, but I will if you provoke me to. Now give me your gun and don't try any funny business; my gun is hammerless with one safety on the firing pin and one in the chamber, so you do the math."

"Okay, be cool, guy," the man said, passing his pistol behind to Melsean who took it and tucked it into his pants. "Now explain to me how you know my name and who sent you."

"Reach into the left pocket of my suit jacket and pull out my wallet and we can go from there."

Melsean reached into his pocket like the man instructed and pulled out his wallet and unfolded it to reveal a New York Police Department shield and badge number with a picture of a man that read *Officer EV Davis*. Melsean put the wallet back and took a step away.

"So, Officer Davis, I assume Detective Lynch sent you to haul me in, huh?"

"No. Actually, I'm here on my own accord."

"Yeah, and what's your angle in this?"

"I figured you were on your way to find the guy that fits your genetic make-up and figured you might need help."

These words shocked Melsean and Isabella because they thought no one knew but them.

"How did you find out about the lab reports? I just received them, so you couldn't have possibly seen it."

"On the contrary," Officer Davis said. "District Attorney Wilson didn't just fax you a copy of the report, she also emailed a copy to Detective Lynch in care of One Police Plaza office. I was down there doing some paperwork on the murder when Lieutenant Klein gave me the documents to pass on to the detective, but he shut me away from the case so hard that I couldn't resist."

"And remind me again why we need your help?" Melsean asked.

"It's clear that Detective Lynch wants to bring you down whether you're guilty or not. I have a band radio in my car, so I'll know if he's in the area and I can warn you. Furthermore, I'm probably the only one in the entire precinct that knows you're innocent and interested in finding the real guilty one."

Melsean took Officer Davis' gun out of his pants and passed it back to the man and they both put their weapons away."

"Okay, Officer Davis."

"Call me EV, Melsean. If we're going to be helping each other, the least we can do is acknowledge each other as friends would."

"I can respect that," Melsean said. "Like I was saying, before we go anywhere, EV, it's only fair that you know what we know, so let me give you the rundown on things."

Melsean brought EV up to speed with what the Doctor at the specimen's lab told them and the dream he had earlier. EV appeared to take it all in stride. He didn't seem the slightest bit bothered by these revelations. Isabella just looked back and forth between the two as they spoke, not wanting to interrupt their dialogue. After everything was said, EV scratched his head for a minute in contemplation, then turned back to the two.

"So, what you're saying is we might be dealing with a beast that is supposedly related to you?"

Melsean and Isabella looked at each other then turned back to EV and nodded their heads in unison.

"That's interesting."

"Well, at least we don't have to worry about Detective Lynch and his sniff hound."

"I wouldn't be too sure of that if I were you."

"What do you mean by that?"

"That's what I was trying to tell you earlier. I called Dr. Benning as well, and he told me that he'd already had a conversation with Detective Lynch. My guess is he's probably on his way to the same place we are."

"I guess we'd better gas our vehicles and get a move on because we just wasted a lot of time politicking."

Both men filled their tanks and headed onto Dark Shadow Pennsylvania.

Twenty-Five

*D*etective Lynch was pulling out of the gate of Isabella's villa when he almost ran Kayman down. He pulled to the shoulder of the road and rolled down his window to talk to the man.

"What's the matter with you? Are you crazy? I could've killed you just now."

"I'm sorry, Officer. My mind was somewhere else just now. I just drove a good distance from Manhattan to see my friend that lives right there and my car conked out on me."

He had caught Detective Lynch's attention. "That house there? You're here to see Isabella, as in Isabella Danpier?"

"Yes, that's her," Kayman said looking at the two men suspiciously. "Is something wrong?"

"Well, son, that's what we're trying to find out now, and we'd appreciate it if you'd give us any information that'll be helpful in this investigation."

"What investigation? You're referring to the case against Melsean in regards to the Sergeant Matthew McCray, right?"

Kayman's question caught Detective Lynch off guard. "Who are you to Isabella and how do you know so much about the Natas investigation?"

"To answer your first question, I'm Isabella's work colleague and best friend, so I share an interest in this case. Also, the investigation's been plastered all over the TV since the murder occurred. Who's not familiar with Melsean's case?"

"Well, apparently you because you failed to mention the murder of Assistant District Attorney Desiree Wilson," Donavan said with a note of hostility and agitation.

"Damn!" Kayman said in a shocked tone. "I know her. She was a good friend of mine and we've had plenty of cases together. What happened to her?"

"I'll tell you what happened to her, you and your friend's sick fucker client happened to her. The son of a bitch raped and sodomized her with a goddamn spiked bat!"

Kayman cringed from the detective's tone. "How can you be sure he did it? Do you have proof?"

The detective looked at Kayman, red-eyed with obvious disgust. "Do I have proof? I have proof that your client is making it his business to kill off everybody close to this investigation and it has to end tonight!"

"Where are you heading, Detective?"

"I'm heading up to Saint Katherine's in Dark

Shadow, Pennsylvania to take your client into custody and your colleague, too, if she tries to obstruct
justice."

"Well, being my car isn't going anywhere
tonight, would you mind if I hitch a rid with you? I'd
like to be there just in case they both need legal
consultation."

"Sure, why not? Your service might be needed
and we don't want to be accused of violating anyone's rights, do we?" He and Sheldon laughed to
themselves, "Hop in the back Mr..."

"Please, call me Kayman," he said as he got in,
closing the door behind him. "If we're going to ride
together, the least we could do is know each other's
names."

"That's true," Donavan said, pulling off of the
shoulder and heading toward the southern parkway
heading north. He reached his hand over the seat
and introduced himself formally. "I'm Detective
Donavan Lynch and the silent guy beside me is
Sheldon." Both men shook hands and became quiet.
Kayman didn't say another word until they got on
the New Jersey Turnpike heading down 13-South.

"So, Detective, I mean Donavan, what made
you join the force in the first place?"

"Actually, my father was a detective and he
wanted me to follow in his footsteps. Back then, I
was the rebellious type, so I kept putting it off."

"What made you finally give in?"

Donavan looked through the rearview mirror
as he talked to Kayman. "My father was murdered by
some punks that strong armed him. Cock suckers

didn't even take his wallet."

"Wow, I'm sorry to hear that," Kayman said, then paused and snapped his fingers. "Wait a second, I remember that case; it was about twelve years ago, wasn't it?"

"Yeah, but it's like it happened just yesterday to me. It actually haunts me everyday. I swore at his funeral that I wouldn't rest or take a day off until I found his killers."

Kayman leaned forward resting his arms over the headrests on both front seats. "I can respect that, Detective. I guess I would do the same thing if the roles were reversed, but I do see a bright side in all of this."

"Oh, and what is that?" Detective Lynch said looking over his shoulder at Kayman.

"I have a feeling you're going to be taking a hell of a long vacation soon."

"Why do you say that?" Sheldon asked while turning to look at the young man behind him as well.

"Hey, I figure a detective of your status and expertise, at least from what I've heard about you, shouldn't have any problem solving that case because you always get your man."

Donavan and Sheldon laughed out loud together. "You know what, I like your style. I'm sure you're right."

"You're damn right, I'm right," Kayman said with a smirk on his face. "Who knows, he might be closer than you think. Sometimes the things we seek the most are right under our noses and we never notice them."

Donavan and Sheldon stopped laughing and thought about what Kayman just said because it definitely made sense and they spent the rest of their journey pondering it.

Twenty-Six

*T*he two cars reached Dark Shadow Pennsylvania at eleven o'clock p.m. and Saint Katherine's was less than five minutes away. Officer EV Davis pulled alongside Melsean and they both lowered their windows.

"Okay, we're almost there. I'm going to take the lead from here since I'm an officer. Whoever's in charge will be more apt to cooperate with us if I do most of the talking. Makes sense?"

Melsean nodded his head as well as Isabella, who appeared to be getting drowsier by the minute.

"Are you all right, Isabella?" EV asked.

"I'm a little fatigued, but I'll snap out of it once we get where we're going."

"Good, because we're going to need all the eyes and ears we have from this point on. Let's get moving." He rolled up his window and pulled off as Melsean drove behind him. Five minutes later, they were turning onto a half-mile driveway that spiraled into Saint Katherine's.

The school was humongous and it resembled the likes of an Irish castle. It was in a world of its own. Along the roof and lower summits were limestone gargoyles that stretched their bodies in animated strike poses.

Isabella looked at it in astonishment, mesmerized by its well-preserved structure.

"Next to having a nightmare, did you know of this place?"

"No. I'm sure I would have remembered something like this."

Isabella hugged herself. "Yeah, because this place definitely freaks me out and we're still on the outside."

Both cars pulled up ten feet away from the front entrance. Storm clouds started to form along with lightening flashes across the skyline, followed by mighty crackles of thunder. They all got out of their vehicles and had one last huddle before approaching the door.

"Okay, here we are," EV said. "Saint Katherine's School of Psycho Dynamic Studies for the Gifted—is it me or does this place freak you out, too?"

"Oh, its definitely not just you," Isabella said. "Let's hurry up and do what we came to do and get out as quickly as possible."

"I'm with you," Melsean said turning to look at EV. "Lead us on."

"Okay, but I just want to say one thing, and I want to hear both of you give me your word that regardless of what goes down tonight, we stick to the plan and don't compromise the mission for any casualties. Okay?" He looked between the both of them. "Are we clear on that?"

"You have my word," Melsean said, and EV looked at Isabella and cleared his throat.

"Fine, I promise. Now can we go in before it starts pouring out here?"

They ran to the door and EV rung the bell. They all cringed from the eerie sound it released. Seconds later, the sound of bolts being moved came from the other side of the door and a woman looking to be in her mid-forties stood in front of them.

"Do you people have any idea what time it is? This is private property and you are trespassing."

"Sorry to have awakened you, ma'am," EV said, taking his position as leader. "I'm Officer EV Davis from New York City Homicide Division and we would like to speak to whomever's in charge of your establishment."

"You're in luck, Mr. Davis. I just so happen to be in charge. Come, I smell rain in the making." She widened the opening of the door and they entered one by one.

She led them through an inner vestibule into a master chamber filled with Renaissance and Neoclassical art dating back to the turn of the seventeenth and eighteenth centuries. She sat them at the heart of a well-lit fireplace.

"You'll have to excuse the fire, but these walls can harbor a devil of a draft," the woman said while reaching for a poker to stoke the flames. "Can I offer you some coffee? I see the poor lady with you can barely keep her eyes open."

"Thank you. You're very kind," Isabella said.

"How would you like your coffee, Officer Davis?"

"Two spoons of sugar and creamer, thank you."

"And what about you two? Oh dear, I don't believe I got your names."

"My goodness!" EV exclaimed. "Where are my manners? This is Isabella Danpier and this here is Melsean Natas."

The woman stared at him for a long time, causing Melsean to become uncomfortable. She then moved in closer to get a better look at him in the light of the fire and then she spoke.

"Yes, now I remember. It's been decades, but you still have your mother's smile."

"You knew my mother?" Melsean asked, unable to hide his enthusiasm.

"Of course, and I know why you're here. Don't worry, I will answer all of your questions, but first I'll get you your coffees and pastries." She left the room.

The storm outside became more intense and they could now hear the rain banging against the bricks of this medieval structure.

"Wow! Did you see that look she just gave you, Melsean?" Isabella asked.

"Yeah. It was kind of creepy at first, but it was a look of recognition. You heard her."

"I don't know. Let's not be precocious in our thinking," EV said, scanning the chamber's inner peripheries for anything strange.

The woman returned with a tray containing a silver coffee pot, cups, spoons, sugar, and a cream dispenser. She also had an assortment of pastries carefully selected to compliment the robust flavor of the fresh coffee. Suddenly, Isabella looked to her left and began to scream while pointing her finger at an unrecognizable silhouette scaling the wall.

"My word, child! Why are you screaming?" the woman asked.

Isabella pointed to the lump of mass hiding behind the window curtains. "There's something moving over there and it ran when I spotted it!"

"Wouldn't that give you the impression that whomever it was obviously fears you just as much as you fear it, if not more?" The old woman moved toward the curtains and pulled them aside. A girl about the age of fifteen with long, jet black hair flowing in long curly locks past her shoulders stood there looking back at them. She had soft features with the cutest set of brown, almond-shaped eyes to match her complexion.

"Young lady, why are you hiding in the dark and scaring our guests?" the lady asked her.

"I heard talking and I got curious, so I came down to see. That lady there scared me, so I hid."

The old lady escorted her over to the guest and introduced her. "This here is Amani, one of my personal favorites here at the school. My name is Sister Katherine Natas, and Amani's my daughter."

Melsean looked between EV and Isabella and they both seemed to be just as shocked as he was to hear her name.

"Are we related? My name just so happens to be Natas as well?"

Katherine looked at him adoringly. She had the appearance of somebody tortured by the grip of nostalgia, only speaking when she could no longer retain her emotions. "I am your mother, Melsean."

This bit of information rocked everybody in the room except for Katherine and Amani. Melsean appeared to be devastated by the hard blow of reality that was pushed on him without so much as a gentle kiss of subtlety.

"You can't possibly be! There's no way in the world! My parents are Adam and Eva Massey!"

"Yes, my love," Katherine said moving closer to him. "They were your parents. They took good care of you for me."

"This is all some insane joke, isn't it?"

"I'm afraid not, Melsean. Do you mean to tell me that it never occurred to you that your last name is different from your parents?"

"Yeah, they told me my mother had me out of wedlock."

"Did you ever ask her for her maiden name or check your birth certificate for that matter?"

Melsean recalled filling out the name *Martin* in the slot for his mother's maiden name slot when he was applying for college, but it never occurred to him that neither his father nor mother shared his name. He sat slumped on the couch, defeated by the uncontrolled flow of truth. However, it was too late to turn back now. He needed to know everything. He looked to Katherine for more answers.

"Why was I led to believe I was a part of a family when I had a family right here? How could you play God with my life?"

"That's exactly what I did," she raved. "I protected my son from the fate of an early grave. I already lost one son to this wretched curse, and I was determined not to lose another unless he killed me first."

"What curse, and what other son did you have? Did I have a brother somewhere? Who is it that you're referring to?"

Katherine closed her eyes and took a few breaths to collect her thoughts. When she felt she had it together, she began to answer Melsean's questions. "Okay, I'm going to answer your questions in the order you presented them. Please do not interrupt me until I'm done and I will do my best to satisfy your curiosity. Fair enough?"

They all nodded in agreement.

"Good. Then let's begin. To answer your first question, the curse I'm referring to extends to the period before time was recorded by man. I'm sure you're familiar with the biblical story of Cain and how he murdered his brother Abel. He was in good favor with God, and God was pleased with him. When God sent Cain away to the city of Nod, not only did God place a mark on him warning others not to murder him, but he also cursed him. He told him that the soil would no longer yield its potential and he would remain a fugitive in the eyes of he Lord—that curse is the curse of Cain.

Melsean cut in for a moment. "Excuse me for interrupting, but I recently had a dream about my having a brother and I remember calling him Cain."

Katherine pondered what he said. "I prayed that hopefully, through the course of time, you would've forgotten about him, but I should have known some of your repressed memories would resurface sooner or later. However, this goes with my answer to your second and third question. You did have an older brother, Melsean. He was my second eldest son and his name was Osiris. Ironic isn't it? Anyway, your brother Osiris never wanted to go out and play with the other children. He always preferred to stay inside with me and help with the chores. You and Osiris had the same father.

Now the oldest, he was something different in himself. His father was a sick bastard, only I didn't know it at the time. I met him through my parents because he was the pastor of our church. Back in those times, a child minded his parents and did what was told, so when my parents sent me over to Pastor Seth's home to do some washing for him, I jumped to it. There were supposed to have been other girls there, but I arrived before them. Pastor Seth told me since I was the first to arrive that I could take the easiest job and clean up his bedroom. He then dumped all of his filthy demon seeds inside me. I was a virgin then." She began to tear. "He ripped me in two as he whispered in my ear that the gates of Heaven had opened up to me. It was a fortunate thing that I was overdeveloped for my age, but it was also very unfortunate because my abnormality caught the devil's eyes."

Pausing for a moment, she quickly scanned their expressions as she placed the steaming cup of coffee to her lips. The rise and fall of her breasts could be calculated as if she intentionally held her emotions at bay. If not for the tears, she would have appeared emotionless. She continued.

"He punched me in every available spot on my body as he raped me to the point of unconsciousness. Luckily, I had a rare condition where I couldn't feel the pain beyond a certain point, and my heartbeat and pulse became so faint that the pastor mistook me for dead. He wrapped me in a crab-infested blanket and buried me under a patch of leaves a few yards from his house. I waited until he left before I crawled out of the blanket and dragged myself home. Once there, I found him trying to convince parents that I never showed up to his home. When I walked in and collapsed in my father's arms, the pastor was shocked with fear. I will never forget that because it marks the first time I'd ever seen him look vulnerable." Her tears continued flowing in a steady stream.

"He was immediately locked away until the day of his trial. When he appeared through the doors of the courtroom, he stopped beside me and winked his eye; that drove the townspeople to a frenzy. It turned out that I wasn't the only nine-year-old that Pastor Seth had an eye for. Several girls came forward that day and gave testimony of the abuse they suffered from him. I was five months pregnant at that time.

"Oh my God," Isabella murmured.

"Oh my God, indeed. My mother damn-near had a stroke when she found out her nine-year-old daughter was having a baby, but the upside of things was that there was enough to convict Pastor Seth of rape and attempted murder. With all that happened, they suggested that it was his word against mine, but my pregnancy was all they needed to sentence him to death by hanging. Pastor Seth was determined not to go to his grave without paying me back for his condemnation. On the day of his execution, he yelled out to me that the demon spawn growing inside of me would avenge his divine will by being at war with every other male child born to me. He said that he damned me with the curse of Cain before they opened the hatch to drop him to his quick demise. Three months later, I gave birth to the devil himself, one month after my tenth birthday, and I've been paying for it ever since."

"I don't understand. When did my brother Osiris get in the picture?" Melsean asked, absorbed in his mother's painful past.

"Be patient, my child. I was just getting there. As you probably know, in those times a woman was not allowed to bear and raise children in the absence of a husband—especially not a ten-year-old girl like me. My parents quickly arranged for me to be married to a man that both of them approved of and considered a friend. His name was Joshua Natas— you and Osiris' father. He was a good man. He took care of me and that..." she searched for the right words to describe him, "that abomination of mine.

Osiris came three years later and he was such a beautiful boy. All the townspeople adored him. My parents wanted to spend every waking moment with their grandchild. Everyone loved my dear Osiris." She smiled, then abruptly switched to a grimace. "Everyone loved Osiris except Cain. Every chance he got to be alone with Osiris, he would try to harm him. My parents said he was just doing what kids his age did because they knew no better. That wasn't the case with him." She paused to reminisce deeper.

"One day while I was frying some fish, I remember it like it was yesterday, I was making Sunday dinner for my family, including my parents. I made hush puppies, macaroni and cheese, cabbage, and homemade candied yams made by my great great grand mama Ida. Osiris was in his crib resting soundly in his room when Cain snuck in without me noticing. By the time I got around to checking on Osiris, his body was cold; Cain had suffocated Osiris with a pillow. I couldn't prove that he did this heinous act, but I did catch him trying to sneak out of the room with the murder weapon and attempt to return it to its rightful place. He then sat back in front of the TV like nothing happened." Her face contorted with vehemence as she spoke of it, but the placid calm was rapidly overtaking her outburst of emotion.

"That little monster killed my baby boy. A mother can feel those kinds of things, you know. I mourned Osiris's death for months and Joshua, may he rest in peace, was so patient with me. Not once did your father pressure me about lying down with him. He waited until my grief subsided and I came to him to make love—that was the day you were conceived, Melsean. Everyday you spent inside my belly, I watched your brother circle me like a vulture circles its prey until it dies so that he can pick it clean to the bone. I gave birth to you exactly nine months to the date of conception. I was attacked by your brother right after I gave birth to you. He was trying to..."

"Kill me," Melsean cut her off. "I know because I've seen it in my nightmares."

"What? You remember that?" she asked amazed.

"Yes, Mom. I remember, but it wasn't your face I seen, but rather my adopted mother's face." He reached for her left arm and rolled up her sweater exposing a long scar across her forearm. "I guess that's what my mind wanted to see."

"I'm sure that you also remember the look on his face because I've been haunted by it everyday since. I knew he wouldn't give up until he killed you and every son born to me, that's why I sent you away. It was pure coincidence that your adopted parents turned out to bear the names Adam and Eva, when you had a psychotic brother who'd been born with the curse of Cain."

"What about my seventh birthday party?"

"That was the last time you saw your brother. It had been seven years since he'd seen you. I thought maybe it was just a childhood phase he was going through, but I was wrong."

"In my nightmare, he bit off my hand, so why

is it still here?" he said twirling his hands in front of him for all of them to see.

"Well, someone did get their hand bitten off, but it wasn't you. It was your father."

"My father? I don't remember that. How did it happen?"

"He was trying to protect you when Cain caught your father's hand in his mouth and bit it off. He then took a chunk out of his neck. It was a miracle that he survived. That was the last time we allowed your brother to see you."

EV and Isabella sat wide-eyed and speechless. It wasn't everyday that a story so supernatural was sprung on them.

"Mrs. Natas, do you think your other son would be willing to kill someone else to get closer to Melsean?" Isabella asked.

"I know he would. He killed Melsean's girlfriend because she was the closest person to him. There's no mistaking that."

"How did you know about me getting arrested for Annette's death?"

"I may be up in age, but I'm not out of touch. I do own a TV. Besides, who do you think retained Isabella and sent that large check?"

"You bailed me out?" Melsean asked surprised.

"Of course."

Isabella cut in. "I saw the name of the institute stamped on the copy of the check I was given, but your signature was illegible. I could only decipher the K and the N."

"Why didn't you say something when I sent

you in the room to get it?" Melsean asked.

"Because I found the fax and talked to the Doctor at the specimen's laboratory. I ended up forgetting to tell you about it."

Melsean left that alone and focused his attention back on his mother. "Why did you send so much money? Wouldn't I have been safer behind bars?"

"No. I paid Isabella all that money because I needed the best to defend my son and right the wrong. Your brother would have used the situation to get at you."

"What could he possibly do, impersonate a cop to get close to me?"

"He doesn't need to impersonate anybody. He's an attorney."

Her statement caused Isabella to spit her coffee back out, choking from it going down the wrong pipe. "I'm sorry, Mrs. Natas, did you say your son is an attorney?"

"Yes, I did."

"What exactly is your son's full name?"

"I'm sorry, didn't I tell you?" his mother asked blankly while sipping her coffee and savoring the last drop.

"No, Mom. You only referred to my brother as *he* or *him*. I was under the impression that his name was Cain."

"No, we only refer to him as Cain because of his actions. We named your brother..."

"Kayman!" yelled a monstrous voice. Kayman revealed himself by stepping out of the shadows of the guest chambers where they were sitting, startling everyone. He stood before them wearing a jet-black outfit with his hands and face protruding with fleshy spikes. He stared Melsean down with the utmost disrespect while clutching a black, leather bag.

"Well, well, well, if it isn't my long, lost brother. I've been searching for you for a very long time. Can you imagine how happy it was to have bumped in to you twelve years ago?"

"I don't know what you're talking about! We've only met earlier today," Melsean said confused.

"I can understand why you'd say that, being we weren't properly introduced. Think back to that day you and your friend decided you were going to dig some old man's pockets. You both were surprised when you found out he was an off-duty police officer."

Melsean knew exactly what he was talking about and his face was a dead giveaway.

"Ah, you remember. I see it in your eyes. Now what exactly did they call that captain?" he asked while tapping his finger on his temple. "Oh, I remember now. It was Captain James Lynch if my memory serves me correctly. Yeah, come to think of it, that was his name before he had an untimely demise."

Isabella and Katherine looked at Melsean in disbelief. Melsean, reading their expressions, especially EV's, became defensive.

"Don't look at me that way. I didn't kill him. Some wild lunatic came from out of nowhere and snapped his neck. I never told the authorities or my parents because I knew they wouldn't have believed me."

They looked at Kayman, who seemed to be enjoying this game, then realized he was being watched. "What? Okay, he didn't do it, but he might as well had. If it wasn't for him starting it, I would have never had to kill the man and his son would have never became a bastard. Then again, now that I think about it, I believe you've met his son Detective Donavan Lynch. Haven't you? He had a hard-on for you, but his first passion was to find the man that killed his father and he never took a day off since then. He told me the story and it just touched my heart. I wanted to do something special for him and give him what he deserved the most."

"Oh, and what's that?" Melsean asked with vehemence.

Kayman stared at Melsean with a blank, impassive expression. "To meet his father's killer, silly. Which reminds me," he raised the black, leather bag, and with his other hand, unzipped it and let the heads of Detective Lynch and Officer Smith fall to the ground and roll toward the fireplace.

Amani and Isabella began to scream uncontrollably, as well as Katherine, who was clutching at her heart as if to keep it from jumping out of her chest. Officer EV Davis threw up all over the floor from the sight of Donavan's eyes staring blankly at them with a look of fright permanently plastered on his face. Melsean stood there stunned, unable to believe that any of this was happening. He hoped to God that what he was seeing was just another bad dream and that he would soon wake up.

"You killed my Annette! Didn't you?"

"Yes, just like I killed Sergeant McCray, Desiree Wilson, and the janitor of her office building. I was going to kill a kid in jail that was scheming on your jewelry, but they called you too soon."

Melsean shook his head. "Wait a minute. You mean to tell me that you were locked up with me?"

"That's what I'm saying, little brother."

"There's no way you could've been there and I didn't see you. I would've remembered seeing you."

"Tell me something, how could you be sure of anything you saw that day? I'm sure mother has told you about my gifts. Besides, who do you think was the person that walked out of the pen with you?"

Melsean recalled one guy being escorted with him to the courtroom, but he disappeared before they reached it. He suddenly became angry. "Why would you kill all of those innocent people? They didn't do anything to you. You could've caught me anytime, the way you tell it."

"That's true, but it's because of mother here," he pointed. "It's her fault that I'm cursed to be a fugitive for life and summoned to tarnish your good name before I kill you. I must admit that they've served their purpose. Now it's your turn," he said as he approached Melsean.

"Please remove yourself from my path, Katherine, and let hell have its way," Kayman said in a flat voice of a hundred men and beasts. EV wiped his mouth off and reached for his forty-caliber pistol. He cocked it back and aimed.

Kayman wagged his finger at the cop and shook his head in disagreement of EV's intentions. "You don't really want to do that. Do you, Officer Davis?"

"How the hell do you know my name?"

"I do believe that my mother just told you that I'm an attorney, so naturally I have a few sources of my own. Who do you think tipped off your precinct in all your murder investigations?"

"You were the anonymous caller on those occasions? How can that be? One was a female and you don't sound like a female."

"How can you be sure what you've seen or heard?" Kayman asked, metamorphosing into a woman, but not just any woman—Melsean's best friend Andy. "I assume my mother didn't get around to explaining that one of my gifts is the ability to shape-change into whatever I want and take on its DNA structure, combined with my own of course."

"Well, that explains why the blood found at the crime scene matched Melsean's DNA," Isabella said.

"How perceptive the little strumpet is, huh?" Kayman said sardonically. "You're so perceptive that you don't even realize you fell in love with my brother because he subconsciously remind you of me."

"That's not true!" Isabella cried.

"What?" EV asked. "Now all of a sudden you're a monster slash psychiatrist? Give me a fucking break!"

"Well, if it isn't the cop that nobody listens to. To whom do I owe the pleasure of your presence?"

"How about me? I can use the reimbursement for the gas and toll money that it took to find your crazy ass."

"I tell you what, I'm going to pay you some advice, officer. It would be wise of you to walk outside that door and just walk away. If you stay, I can't be responsible for your safety."

"Gee, now where have I heard that before?" EV asked while holding his gun steady.

"EV, no!" Melsean cried out stepping between the two of them.

"Get out of the way, Melsean. Let's be done with this."

"No, EV. This is between me and Kayman. I appreciate your loyalty, but I have to do this alone."

"Hello? Is it just me or is anybody else in here aware that this guy is a demon?"

"No. Melsean, is right," Katherine interjected. "This war between brothers started millenniums ago through Cain and Abel. The only way to close this chapter and defeat the curse is for Abel to finally slay Cain. That's what God's mark on Cain represented."

"So, what are we supposed to do in the meantime?" Isabella asked.

Amani walked up to Isabella, grabbed her hand in hers, and gave it a firm squeeze before responding. "We are their witnesses."

"Witnesses? I can't believe this! Melsean, be careful, honey!"

Melsean pulled out his gun and gave it to his mother to hold. "The curse must stop here," he stated as he and Kayman circled around each other, appearing to feel each other out.

"You don't know how long I've waited for this moment, little brother. You can't even imagine spending every waking day of your life thinking and hating someone you barely knew and not understand why. But no more—it ends tonight!" He then lashed out at Melsean and tossed him across the room.

Kayman darted after Melsean, reaching him just as he landed and gripped him by the neck. Melsean felt the fleshy spikes puncturing his skin as Kayman attempted to squeeze the life out of him. EV stood beside Katherine and anxiously watched Melsean being beat to a pulp. He couldn't bear standing there and not being able to do anything. He turned his head to look at Katherine and noticed that she was rather calm for a woman who watched as her two sons fought to the death.

"Are you sure there's nothing we can do to help Melsean?" EV asked her.

"The only thing you could possibly do is witness history in the making. Kayman is very strong and would have no trouble killing you, even if you happened to get a shot off. Kayman would simply morph into something to deflect the bullet and then he would do unspeakable things to you. I'm sure you've seen his work."

"If I can't take him, how do you expect Melsean to? He's almost half my size."

"What you're failing to realize is that Melsean and Kayman carry the same bloodline through me. Seth only provided the evil nature in Kayman as

Joshua provide the positive in Melsean and Osiris—I provide the strength, so they're equally matched."

"Then why the hell is Kayman kicking Melsean's ass?" Isabella added.

"It might be the fact that he's intimidated by Kayman's monstrous appearance. He's going to have to get over that if he intends to win."

Kayman swung at Melsean's face, but missed his mark and smashed his fist into the bricks. That gave Melsean enough time to regroup and develop a strategy against him. He was very strong and his features were no comfort to Melsean, either. He wasn't sure what he feared most, his brother's strength or his appearance.

After seeing as much as she could stand, Katherine intervened and began coaching Melsean. "Melsean, why aren't you fighting back?"

"He's not a regular man, Mom! I don't know where to begin evening up this match."

"Don't worry, little brother. It's going to end just as fast as it started." Kayman punched Melsean on the right side of his body and fractured one of his ribs. The sound made a sickening crunch.

Katherine cried as she struggled to watch the onslaught. She loved both of her sons, but was torn by the dark path of her eldest, even knowing that he had to be put to rest so that the curse of Cain would die with him.

Kayman picked up Melsean, placing him sideways over his shoulders, and proceeded to literally break him in half. His plan was to snap Melsean like a twig.

Katherine knew she had to do something to bring some advantage to the good son. "Melsean, listen to me and listen to me good! You and Kayman have the same strengths. Never mind his appearance, that's just a smokescreen to intimidate you."

"It doesn't feel like any smokescreen!" Melsean said wincing from pain.

"Listen to me, your brother has the curse of Cain, which means he has to have the mark God gave him somewhere on his body. Find that mark and that should give you all the advantage you need."

"What exactly am I looking for?"

"You'll know it when you see it."

"Thanks a lot! You've been a big help!" Melsean said sarcastically. He reached up with his left index and middle fingers and pressed them into the back of Kayman's ear, hitting his pressure point and causing Kayman to drop him. Melsean then began to focus on ripping Kayman's clothes off.

Every time the monstrous figure swung, kicked, or leaped at Melsean, he would duck and rip off a good portion of his brother's clothes, exposing another area of skin. About twelve ducks later, Melsean had Kayman stripped down to his boxer briefs, and even that was too much for any to have seen. Behind the fleshy spikes that covered his body were muscles on top of more muscles. He reminded Melsean of a fictional, evil, action figure, only he was limber and maneuvered like none Melsean came in contact with before.

"I thought you said there was a mark on his body?" Melsean asked.

"There has to be a mark on his body some-where. You didn't check him everywhere. He still has clothes on."

"He's only wearing drawers, Mom. You expect me to take those off?"

"That may be our only hope, honey!" Isabella yelled. "Do what your mother said!"

Kayman tried to rush Melsean and scoop him off the floor, but Melsean dipped and shot two right crosses that sent Kayman crashing to the ground. In the same motion, Melsean grabbed Kayman's under-wear from both sides and pulled them down. He still couldn't find anything remotely similar to a mark; not his ears, nose, feet, armpits, nothing. There was, however, one place that appeared to harbor the most spikes that was by far longer and sharper than the rest on his body. Melsean now knew what to do. He waited for Kayman to get up from the floor.

Kayman reached down and pulled his briefs back up slowly, careful not to rip them from his spiked phallus. "Gee, I didn't know you cared, little brother. However, thanks but no thanks. I don't swing that way."

"Just come on and fight, you sick bastard!"

"Those are very cute words coming from a dead man. I'll be sure to have them carve that on your headstone after you're gone."

"Well, I'm sure you've heard this cliché before, big bro—age before beauty, so after you. I insist."

Kayman became frustrated and charged Melsean with his head down in blind rage. Melsean timed him perfectly and waited until Kayman was right on him before stepping aside and shooting a flurry of quick jabs, tight hooks, and rabbit punches at various angles of Kayman's head. Kayman shook the punches off and donkey kicked Melsean across the room and into their baby sister Amani. Alarmed, Melsean quickly pulled himself up and checked her for injuries. She had fallen pretty hard on her head and wasn't coming to.

"That one is going to cost you, Kayman!" Melsean growled.

"Hey, bet next time she'll stay out of the way," Kayman chided. "I don't like her anyway."

"You're dead, Kayman!"

"Not if you keep fighting the way you are. I know what you're looking for and you're never going to find it. You might as well stop fighting the inevitable and die like the coward you are."

"Now you're just getting ahead of yourself." *Dammit, that's it*, he thought to himself. *I know what to do now.* Melsean reached out and pulled Isabella to him. He then kissed her passionately and groped her in all the right places causing Kayman's blood to boil.

"What the hell do you think you're doing, Melsean?" Kayman asked, clenching his fists even tighter.

Melsean separated his kiss with Isabella with a big smacking sound as he turned to Kayman. "I now see why you hate me so much. I guess I'd be pissed off if my younger brother was more handsome than I was and took my girlfriend—I mean ex-girlfriend. She has a burning desire to be with his baby brother."

"Please, she didn't know you were my baby brother."

"True, but she knew a sexy beast when she saw one, and you, my brother, are no sexy beast."

Kayman became pissed and was about to explode any second. He was staring between Melsean and Isabella with pure unadulterated hate for the two of them.

Melsean decided to drive the last nail into the coffin. "Let's be real, it's no secret that I get the best of everything over you; God loves me more, Mom loves me more, and now I've got your woman."

Isabella and EV looked from each other to Melsean then to the angered Kayman—both wondering what the hell Melsean was trying to do. He was definitely going to get them all killed now.

Kayman snarled like a wild animal and charged both Melsean and Isabella in a raging manner. "Ill kill you both!" he snarled.

Reacting out of pure instinct, Melsean clumsily pushed Isabella out of the way and onto the floor, sending her reeling backward on her derrière, and in the same motion he scooped Kayman up by his crotch and shoulder. With every ounce of his strength, he raised his brother in the air and earth-slammed him onto the crown of his head, crushing the soft mole that harbored the mark of God's wrath. Kayman died instantly.

Melsean collapsed out of fatigue and pain. He held his chest and could feel the swelling around his ribcage. EV helped Isabella from the floor and the four of them gathered around Melsean. His mother gently placed her hand on his shoulder and looked at him with loving eyes.

"I had no doubt, Son. God was with you."

"I'm glad you knew it," he said shaking his head and lifting his eyes to the heavens. His lips motioned "thank you" and he winked knowing that the same father that loved and protected him all this time had indeed shown favor in him. He pulled Isabella close to him with her nose touching his. "Are you all right?"

"I am now," she said, gently kissing him. "We need to get you to the doctor."

Melsean looked at EV. "You can put your pistol away now. I don't believe we're in any more danger."

EV looked at Kayman's body and shrugged while returning his gun to its holster. "Just making sure. You've got to admit that I had your back!"

"Yes, you did," Melsean said accepting EV's hand and allowing him to pull him from the floor.

Epilogue

Isabella kneeled down in the dirt and planted seeds and shrubs for Katherine's garden, which surrounded the structure of her school. Amani was on her knees beside her in a pair of dirt and grass-stained overalls and a light colored plaid shirt three times her size over it. She seemed so happy since *that* night. Isabella planted the last shrub in the fresh, tilled soil, then asked Amani to help her get up. It was too much of a struggle to lift herself off the ground—pregnancy had been known to have that effect.

Isabella left her firm three months after the incident, staying only long enough to see to it that all of the charges against Melsean were dropped. That was not a problem with the help of the evidence ascertained by the late District Attorney Desiree Wilson, Detective Donavan Lynch, and Officer Sherman Smith. Of course, Officer EV Davis made the difference with his outstanding testimony. Channel 21 held a public apology on-air for Melsean, not to mention an unconfirmed amount of settlement money for slander and defamation of character, and news reporter Jasmine Diaco gave her Oscar-winning performance.

Melsean hadn't talked much about the incident nor did he allow it to be discussed in his presence. Apparently, a part of him died when his brother did. He spent a lot of time with his mother and he absolutely adored his sister Amani. He usually made it his business to drop her off and pick her up from school. He knew that she'd later complain about it because no teen wanted their big brother dropping off and picking them up from high school. Then again, deep in her heart she understood his reasons for being overprotective and she was just as anxious to spend time with him.

Isabella sold her house in the Hamptons and moved in with Melsean and his family in Dark Shadow, Pennsylvania. It was actually Katherine's idea. She said she needed an attorney to handle the legal affairs of her business and Isabella was more than happy to join her lucrative operation. The children took a liking to Isabella from the first visit. Some harbored the ability of psycho kinesis where others were blessed with the gift of clairvoyance. Katherine had a PhD in Psychology and Psycho Dynamic studies, so not only did she deal with the extraordinary, she dealt with those with learning impediments and counseled them on how to adapt to normal society.

A few months later, Isabella gave birth to a healthy baby boy, weighing in at nine pounds and six ounces. She named him Osiris in tribute to Melsean's late brother. Officer EV Davis and Isabella's best friend April, who were now dating each other, became the Godparents of Osiris. They met at the family's Fourth of July cookout and had been insep-arable ever since.

Melsean still had nightmares about his brother returning to tie up loose ends, but never shared those dreadful visions with anyone. It was hard enough coming to terms that he had a brother, but being told that he alone had to kill him in order to end the curse that allegedly stretched to the begin-ning of man's existence was too much of a mental burden. There was no rational way to look at such a fate; he simply had to close his eyes, dive into the problem, and pray he didn't hit something hard.

The summers in Dark Shadow were pleasant. They weren't quite as cool as the constant sea breeze encountered in the Hamptons from the Long Island Sound, but they sufficed.

Melsean turned out to be the perfect father. Katherine said he was a spitting image of his father Joshua. Isabella would have never suspected that one day could determine a lifetime of happiness. Her experience with Melsean started as a one-night stand and developed into a full fledge relationship over night. If that wasn't a fairytale in the making, nothing was.

Melsean and Isabella married exactly one year after the birth of Osiris to ensure that his progeny carried on the family legacy. Their second child was born almost three years behind Osiris and, despite the clash between Melsean and his big brother, he decided to name his second child Kayman as a way of leaving something pure in his memory. Isabella loved the idea and Kayman was named at the time of his birth.

Orisis took to his baby brother from the beginning. He would spend hours holding his hand or playing peek-a-boo to entertain him, but Kayman never smiled. He'd just stare at the toddler as if his presence puzzled him. None of this struck either parent as odd behavior. They wrote it off as typical child behavior like Melsean's parents did with their children so many years ago. It wasn't until Kayman's sixth birthday that everything began to change.

Isabella was at the front door of the Mansion, welcoming the parents of children who came to attend Kayman's party. She escorted the families to the backyard with the help of April and Amani. Melsean was working the grill with some T-bones, roasted corn on the cob, and barbeque beef ribs. He was entertaining the fathers of the children with his outstanding culinary skills. Melsean had finished the burgers and hotdogs for the children and was now ready to take care of the parents.

Isabella walked over to Melsean and gave him a long, affectionate kiss and wrapped her arms around his waist. She then stared over his shoulder at the children as they played Freeze Tag, but Osiris and Kayman were nowhere to be found.

"Melsean, have you seen the birthday boy?"

"Not since I set up the grill. Why?"

"Most of his friends have already arrived, but he's not out here playing with them."

"Did you ask Osiris?"

"That's my point. He's not out here, either."

Melsean asked EV to watch over the grill while he helped Isabella look for Kayman and Osiris. They went into the house and searched the first floor, starting with the furthest point which was also Kayman's favorite part of the house. They searched the kitchen, living room, guest chambers, dining room, and bathrooms, but nothing turned up. They checked every room on the second and top floors, but still neither of the boys could be found.

"What about the basement?" Katherine asked, stepping into the room and stopping in front of Isabella. "Did you check there?"

Isabella began to panic and she felt her heart getting heavy with pain for the obvious. "No, Melsean! Not again! I can't do it. I won't do it!"

Melsean shook her by her shoulders. "Get a grip on yourself, Bella. Let's not jump to any conclusions."

"Honey, I didn't know this place had a basement. I'm scared. Something isn't right."

The basement door was located on a blocked-off corner in the laundry room on the west wing of the house. Isabella would have never found this door on her own, and what troubled her more was that she had no idea what other hidden secrets lay within the confinement of this castle-like mansion.

Isabella opened the door and called to both children, but neither responded. She tried again but received the same cold silence. "You said they might be down here, but they're not answering. Why won't they answer?"

Melsean wrapped his arms around her and tried to calm her down, but it was going to take more than a hug and a few soothing words to ease Isabella's mind. She was worried about her children and so was Melsean, but someone had to be brave for the rest of them.

"Calm down, Isabella. Just because they didn't answer doesn't mean they're in trouble. Besides, we haven't even checked downstairs yet. Don't write them off so early in the search."

Isabella nodded in agreement and allowed herself to relax a bit. Melsean led the way down the stairs followed by Isabella and Katherine. It was gloomy and musky down there and everything about the place gave Isabella the creeps. Her mind kept flashing images of Osiris standing over Kayman and vice versa. She respected Katherine because there was no way in the world she could handle losing a child, let alone by the hands of her other child that happened to be psychotic. She knew that she'd literally die if anything happened to either one of them.

Isabella looked at the expression on Katherine's face and could see the anxiety building up as they moved further through the basement. Melsean stopped abruptly, causing Isabella to run into him.

"Why did you stop like that?"

"Shhh," Melsean said, waving his hand to tell them to stay quiet and wait for him to give them the signal to follow. He moved on through the tunnel while Isabella and his mother watched from a distance. Melsean heard something stirring behind a stack of boxes and was determined to find out what it was. He made his way closer and closer to the noise and then rounded the boxes and stopped in mid stride with a stunned expression. Isabella's blood froze because of Melsean's expression. When he finally snapped out of it, he motioned for Isabella and Katherine to join him, but they were afraid to see what lay behind the boxes. Melsean motioned again for them to join him and they began to approach him slowly.

As Isabella approached, she prayed and asked God not to make her go through what Katherine had to because that was a pain that no mother should ever have to endure. When she got to Melsean, he pressed his left index and middle fingers to her lips and guided her around the boxes. The site brought tears to her eyes.

Kayman and Osiris were nestled together on a bed of newspapers, sleeping soundly. Their bodies formed a circle around a litter of baby kittens that appeared to have been abandoned. They were lightly crying for something to eat.

"Ah, isn't that the cutest thing you've ever seen?" Isabella asked Katherine.

"It most certainly is," Katherine cooed.

"Where do you think these orphan cats came from?"

"Probably came in through an underground chamber. The cat was pregnant and in need of a nice, cozy place to have its litter."

"Do you intend on keeping them or will you send them to the pound?"

"Well, I won't say the thought didn't cross my mind, but I think the children might enjoy some company around this dreary, old estate."

Melsean and Isabella picked up the kids and carried them upstairs. Katherine trailed behind, carrying the five furry friends of her grandsons. When Kayman woke up, he was greeted with a special birthday song by all of the guests as Osiris hugged him and held him ever so close to his heart. Osiris and Kayman grew to be close friends, and they personified the true essence and definition of brotherly love as intended for all siblings.